THE
COWBOY'S
Reluctant Bride

VALERIE COMER

Greenwords Media

Valerie Comer Bibliography

Urban Farm Fresh Romance

0. Promise of Peppermint (ebook only)
1. Secrets of Sunbeams
2. Butterflies on Breezes
3. Memories of Mist
4. Wishes on Wildflowers
5. Flavors of Forever
6. Raindrops on Radishes
7. Dancing at Daybreak
8. Glimpses of Gossamer
9. Lavished with Lavender

Christmas in Montana Romance

1. More Than a Tiara
2. Other Than a Halo
3. Better Than a Crown

Farm Fresh Romance

1. Raspberries and Vinegar
2. Wild Mint Tea
3. Sweetened with Honey
4. Dandelions for Dinner
5. Plum Upside Down
6. Berry on Top

Saddle Springs Romance
(Montana Ranches Christian Romance)

1. The Cowboy's Christmas Reunion
2. The Cowboy's Mixed-Up Matchmaker
3. The Cowboy's Romantic Dreamer
4. The Cowboy's Convenient Marriage
5. The Cowboy's Belated Discovery
6. The Cowboy's Reluctant Bride

Garden Grown Romance
(Arcadia Valley Romance)

1. Sown in Love (ebook only)
2. Sprouts of Love
3. Rooted in Love
4. Harvest of Love

Riverbend Romance Novellas

1. Secretly Yours
2. Pinky Promise
3. Sweet Serenade
4. Team Bride
5. Merry Kisses

valeriecomer.com/books

J ericho!" Sawyer Delgado bellowed his nephew's name as the kid slid off the rail fence amid a frenzy of bawling calves and clouds of dust. "Nooo!"

Pivoting Debonair into the melee, Sawyer fixed his gaze on the spot where the child-size Stetson had disappeared. The wiry pinto cut between dozens of five-hundred-pound calves as Sawyer hung on, heart in his throat. How could this have happened? The five-year-old knew better. Who'd even let the boy near the branding pens? And where was his father, Sawyer's brother Kade?

Totally oblivious, that's where.

Sawyer broke through the corral dust and pulled Debonair to a halt.

His nephew grinned up at him from a closed-off chute, his eyes bright with excitement. "Uncle Sawyer! Those calves are *crazy!*"

They were. Sawyer willed his heart rate to slow down, but superimposed on the boy was a vision of what could have been: Jericho's body battered by heavy hooves, his skull broken, blood everywhere.

He closed his eyes for a brief moment, but that was even worse, because there was no reality to block the nightmare of his buddy's horrific rodeo accident a few weeks back.

Sawyer forced his breathing to steady and stared out at the mountains beyond his father's western Montana ranch. When he could trust his voice, he turned back to his nephew. "You okay, Jer?"

The boy frowned in confusion. "Yeah, why?"

"You scared me when you jumped off the fence." Nothing had ever frightened Sawyer Delgado before that final rodeo. "I thought you'd fallen in with the calves." The calves that were now milling on the other side of the corral, far from Debonair.

"Sawyer!" yelled Kade. "Get over here, and hold this steer!"

Debonair danced in place as Sawyer pinned the boy with a glare. "Stay outside the pens. All the way outside."

"I'm safe here. See, there's a gate."

"Outside."

Jericho rolled his eyes and clambered over the rails to the grass beyond. He raised his eyebrows as though to ask if his surly uncle was happy now.

Sawyer nodded. "Stay there." Then he reined Debonair back into the corral where Trevor and Kade held a rebellious calf in the vaccination chute.

"Quit your sightseeing, and get in here," Trevor

growled, leaning his entire weight against the gate while the calf tried to break free. "You're here to work."

Sawyer looped Debonair's reins over a post and jumped in, freeing Trevor to hop over the rails to load the syringe with the four-way solution. Trevor reached through the chute's rails, lifted a flap of skin on the calf's shoulder, and plunged the needle in.

The steer went ballistic, kicking and bawling, but Sawyer kept the pressure tight on the gate at its heels until Kade opened the head gate and the calf thundered out to join his buddies.

Kade slammed the head gate shut and eyed Sawyer. "What were you doing? That calf nearly shoved through the head gate while you were off gallivanting."

Sawyer skewered his brother with a look. "From here, it looked like Jericho had fallen into the calf pen." If he had kids, he'd take much better care of them. Keep them far from danger.

Kade pivoted, shading his eyes against the October sun. "Is he okay?"

"Yeah." Sawyer took a deep breath. "He'd hopped into the exit chute over there to get a closer look."

The older brother shrugged and turned toward his horse. "He knows to stay out of the way." Kade swung onto Bowen. "I'll get the next calf if you watch the head gate, Trev."

Trevor filled the syringe and set it on the table outside the chute. "Ready." He scrambled over the rails.

Did no one around here take safety seriously? One misstep, and Jericho could have been badly injured or even killed. Mom should keep her grandkids safe in the house on days like today.

Sawyer shoved aside the inconvenient memory of himself as a kid, far more dare-devilish than Jericho likely dreamed of. He'd hopped right in amongst the calves more than once before darting back out, laughing all the way. He was lucky he'd survived.

The mirage of Ace's accident began to sift over this day's reality, but Sawyer slid a memory of Anna Winter in front of it. Sometimes that helped block the ugliness, until he remembered how she'd quit taking his calls.

"Quit spacing out!" bellowed Kade. "Get the gate open."

Sawyer blinked, willing the present to win over the past in any form. He surged up the rails then dropped behind the calf and clanged the rear gate shut as Trevor slammed the head gate and Kade slid off his mount, Bowen. Somehow, he managed to keep his mind in the game, not daring a glance toward his young nephew, not daring another trip down memory lane.

Finally his sister-in-law Cheri approached the corral, calling lunch time. The three brothers hooked their horses' reins outside the corral and stripped off their gloves.

Cheri stretched to give Kade a kiss on his scruffy cheek. He wrapped an arm around her waist as they led the way toward the ranch house, Jericho's hand clasped in his dad's free one.

Trevor glanced at Sawyer, falling into step beside him. "Man, are you okay? You're not the same since you quit the rodeo."

"I'm fine." Liar. "Just got a scare with Jericho there."

"Nothing used to scare you." Trevor laughed and clouted Sawyer's shoulder.

"I know." He took a deep breath. "Guess I grew up." He'd mentioned Ace's accident to his parents to let them know why he was back at Eaglecrest, finished with the circuit for good. No one needed the details.

Sawyer had just reached the back steps when his phone chimed with an incoming text. He pulled the device out of his pocket and stared at it for a moment, barely aware of the door shutting behind his brothers.

Anna?

As though just thinking about her had conjured her up. But why now, after three months?

He'd tried to convince himself her disappearance didn't matter. That he didn't even care. She was hardly his first, uh... relationship. But he should have known better than to get involved with someone back home. Buckle bunnies along the circuit chased rodeo cowboys for the fun and the glory. They had no expectations.

Anna wasn't one of them.

He'd been swept away with her flirty responses to his teasing when he'd been in town for Trevor and Denae's June wedding. It had been fun to needle his brothers at first, but he'd really liked her. She was different. They'd gotten together a few times over the course of a week or two, texted and called for a few weeks after that, then nothing. As far as he could tell, she'd left Saddle Springs in the rearview mirror, since no one seemed to have heard from her. Until today.

Sawyer wasn't accustomed to being ghosted. It was usually him dishing it out. But he couldn't swallow the hope that gurgled up at the thought she was back.

Sawyer, we need to talk.

Not a smiley face in sight. Ominous, and completed unlike the teasing texts they'd shared in early summer. He'd rather talk than text, but when he tapped her number, it went straight to voicemail. Okay, fine. He'd do it her way.

Hey, beautiful. I've missed you. As evidenced by the column of texts he'd sent her since her last response in mid-July.

This time, however, she responded immediately. *I hear you're in Saddle Springs. I'm here for two days. When can I meet you at the fairgrounds?*

Would Sawyer be able to keep focused on the afternoon shots? He'd have to, with a reward like this one waiting for him.

ANNA WINTER WRAPPED her bulky sweater around her torso and tied the sash against the cool October evening. The waning sunshine provided little warmth. Her cardigan could keep most of the external chill out, but it did nothing to thaw the ice in her core.

Seeing Sawyer Delgado again wasn't likely to melt her heart as sight of him had done when they first met. The bold cowboy had been the answer to her very selfish prayer. Now that she was actually praying to a God she was trying to get to know, she fervently wished He'd dumped a cold shower on her that June day.

He hadn't.

She paced toward the riverbank, her hiking boots crunching through fallen leaves in vibrant colors. Blue flashed as a Steller's jay took wing across the river, squawking indignantly at being disturbed.

A black truck displaying the Eaglecrest emblem rattled across the nearby bridge.

Anna wrapped her arms tighter around herself and closed her eyes. *God? I could use a boatload of help here. I know it's my mess, but... please help me.* She watched as the truck turned into the fairgrounds parking lot and pulled up beside her car.

Sawyer jumped out of the cab, his gaze already fixed on hers as he slammed the truck door and started toward her.

He was gorgeous.

She allowed herself a moment to appreciate his total masculine look from brown Stetson to scuffed boots with shades of denim in between, split with a brass-buckled belt. But his face... that was what she'd missed most. His square jaw with its rough scruff, the crooked nose, the inset of his intense eyes.

Anna turned away to break the connection. What had she been thinking, meeting him again? It would have been best to do this by email, but she didn't know how to reach him that way. Or text. But the thought of tapping out the entire message had seemed too daunting. Neither method would have delivered her package.

No. She was doing the right thing. She'd confess. Then they'd talk like two mature adults. He'd sign the papers she'd brought, and he'd drive back over that bridge while she turned the other way.

They'd never see each other again, and that was for the best.

"Anna?"

She took a step away as she turned, arms still in protective mode. "Hi, Sawyer."

His eyes caressed her. "You look great. I've missed you." But there was hesitation in his dusky voice.

Totally her fault, showing up three months after their last communication. He was right to be a little wary, but that was better than the anger she deserved. The anger that was sure to come.

She raised her chin slightly. "I, um, have something to tell you."

He scanned her quickly before meeting her eyes again. "Oh?"

Suspicious, was he? He had a right to be. "I... I'm pregnant."

Sawyer reeled back a step as though she'd slapped him. "No way," he breathed.

"I'm sorry. I should have known better..." The thing was, she *had* known better. She'd taken a gamble she now regretted.

He shook his head. "It took two."

It definitely had, and those were memories she'd like to erase. "I need to put the baby up for adoption. I shouldn't have taken a chance. Shouldn't have... you know." She clenched her sweater tighter. "I have papers for you to sign. This doesn't need to affect you at all."

Arms crossed over his jean jacket as his stance widened. "No."

Tears welled in her eyes. Dratted hormones. "What? Why?" She hated how weak her words came out even as her gaze locked onto his.

"I'm not making a snap decision here, Anna. You've had a bit of time to think about this." Those eyebrows rose into his thick hair. Dark eyes pierced hers. "How long, exactly, have you known?"

"Late July," she whispered.

"Before I came home that time and tried, repeatedly, to get in touch with you."

Anna chomped on her lip until she felt the pain of it. "Yes."

"I can count to nine as well as anyone else. You're what, four months along?"

She nodded.

"So there's no rush to make a decision. A few weeks won't matter."

"I can't stay."

"Sure, you can."

"No, I have a job in Bozeman—"

"I'll offer you a job here. What are you making? I'll pay you more than that, and your medical expenses besides."

Anna lurched back a step as she stared at him. "What? No." Whatever he was offering, she wasn't taking it.

"Mom's been talking about hiring someone to take over some of the office duties for the ranch. Cheri's too busy."

"But then..."

Sawyer leaned in a little, his dark eyes sharp. "Then

she'd know? Yeah, she would. She and Dad will know, anyway. Because I'll tell them."

"No..." It was hard enough without that. Why did he think she'd quit her job at the Branding Iron and left Saddle Springs?

He grimaced. "It's not like they think I'm an angel, Anna. I've done my best to flaunt my indiscretions in front of my family, but you know what? I'm done with all that. I'm back at Eaglecrest for good, and I'll do the right thing."

Anna shook her head frantically. "This isn't the right thing. Signing those papers is. Right now."

Sawyer stepped closer and grasped her arms firmly but gently. "Look at me, Anna."

She didn't want to. She wanted to either tear herself loose and flee or throw herself into his strong arms. But she forced herself to meet his gaze. Oh, those eyes.

"You want my cooperation? It comes at a cost."

Everything always did, but any price he demanded was too high.

"You come to Eaglecrest. There's an empty apartment, so don't worry about that part. I'm not asking you to move in with me."

Her face heated.

"Give me at least one month. No, until after Christmas. If we can't come to an agreement on a different plan by December thirty-first, I'll sign your papers, and you can do whatever you want. I'll still pay all the medical expenses for... our baby."

That left her with several months on her own in the new year before the birth. But he was asking for a similar amount of time now. Time in which she'd face his family's accusations and see him every day. She couldn't. She just couldn't. Anna tilted her chin up, trying for defiance. "Or what?"

"I'm pretty sure a birth mom can't release a baby for adoption without the father's consent. Don't even try to test me. I'll block you. I promise."

Those dark eyes did not waver. How could he know about adoption laws? Did he have more babies stashed around the state? But a guy who had the nerve to ride wild mustangs had little to fear from a weak woman like her. She'd build a cage for her heart and lock it away. By the time March was over, she'd be on her own again. Without Sawyer, without the baby, but wiser. By far.

"You leave me little choice."

"I know," he said simply, releasing her, then pulled out his phone and tapped it. "Mom?" But his gaze was riveted on Anna's. "I've found an assistant for you."

CHAPTER 2

Sawyer parked his truck beside the little white car and hopped out. Anna bent her head over the steering wheel, and he could see her shoulders quaking. Had he made the right call, forcing her hand like he'd done? Well, she'd tried to force his first. There was no way he was going to roll over and play dead. Not on something this important.

He opened the car door, and she looked up at him. She was beautiful even with red-rimmed eyes. "Ready?" He extended his hand to her.

Anna glowered at him then pushed his hand aside as she exited the car. "This is stupid. Just sign the papers, and let me go. Please."

"No."

"You've got nothing to gain." She slammed the car door with a bit more force than necessary.

"On the contrary. I have everything to gain."

Anna's gaze flew to meet his. "I fail to see—"

"I know." He grinned, though it was difficult to affect nonchalance with so much at stake.

The evening sun hovered on the horizon up the valley and cast long shadows on the ranch yard. The exterior light flicked on at his parents' house, and the front door opened.

Show time.

Sawyer should be used to eating crow by now. He'd screwed up often enough, but this one put any earlier escapades to shame. That he knew of, anyway.

Anna glanced toward the doorway outlining both his parents' forms and huddled deeper into her sweater. "Sawyer, please."

"Sweetheart—"

"Don't sweetheart me." Eyes flashing, she straightened as the words shot out.

He preferred the fire to the despair. He'd prefer flirting even more, but that wasn't likely to happen any time soon. He put his hand on the small of her back to nudge her toward the house. Of course, she shifted away, but at least she started walking.

"Dad, Mom, this is Anna Winter. I'm not sure if you remember her..."

Mom gave Sawyer a quick questioning look then focused on Anna. "Hi, Anna. You used to work at the Branding Iron, right? And I remember seeing you at Trevor and Denae's wedding."

Anna swallowed visibly. "Yes, that's me."

"Welcome to Eaglecrest. Sawyer tells me you're in need of a job?"

"Not real—"

"She is," Sawyer cut in. "But it's a long story."

Dad stepped aside, tugging Mom's hand. "Come on in, and let's hear it. We'll put on a pot of decaf."

Was coffee okay for developing babies? Even decaffeinated? "Anna would probably prefer herbal tea."

"Decaf sounds great." Anna glowered at him.

He'd have to do some research before making an issue of it. There were probably all kinds of things she should be avoiding. He'd make sure she knew about them.

Sawyer followed as his parents led the way to the back of the house where the sunset shone gloriously through the expansive glass of the breakfast room. How had Sawyer ever managed to spend so much time away from Eaglecrest in recent years? He'd been so full of himself, too good for the ranch, too high on testosterone.

Dad dumped stale coffee grounds and started a fresh pot while Mom pulled a container of Ruthie's pumpkin chocolate chip muffins from the fridge and arranged a few on a plate.

Anna looked over her shoulder at Sawyer, and he gestured toward the table. "Have a seat." He pulled out a chair for her, and she scowled at him. He leaned close and whispered, "You'll be fine."

"Easy for you to say," she growled back in a low voice.

"You think so?" He raised his eyebrows as he took the seat next to her. "That's where you're wrong."

His mom set the muffins on the table and slid into a chair, glancing uncertainly between them. "I'm not sure what Sawyer's told you about the position I'm looking to fill, Anna."

Anna levered him the stink eye. "Not much, honestly."

Awkward.

"Okay. It's fairly general office work at about twenty-five hours a week. You'll need to be proficient with spreadsheets and website updates. I'd also like someone to file brands and maintain our extensive crop and herd database." Mom's gaze on Anna was steady. "The biggest issue I've found in interviewing potential candidates is the commute up from Saddle Springs, especially in winter. Working remotely isn't a viable option."

"That won't be a problem," Sawyer cut in. "Anna will be living in Kade's old apartment above the garage."

"But..." sputtered Anna.

"Thought *you* were figuring on moving out there." Dad leaned on the end of the kitchen island and crossed his arms, eyebrows raised at Sawyer.

"I'll stay in the house for now. Anna needs the space more than I do."

"Look, I can't do this." Anna surged to her feet, the chair scraping back on the tile floor. "I'm a waitress, not an office worker. I have a perfectly good job in Bozeman."

His parents exchanged a long look. The coffee pot gurgled. "Take anything in your coffee, Anna?" Dad turned back to the kitchen and plucked four mugs from the cupboard.

She sank back into her chair. "Just a little cream, thanks."

Looked like she wasn't going to bolt this minute, after

all. Sawyer reached for a muffin, split it, and buttered it before offering it to Anna. She mumbled her thanks, and he repeated the process for himself. The flavor was amazing. His family was so lucky to have Ruthie cooking for them and the hired men. Besides, he could use some sustenance to ground him for the upcoming conversation.

With the mugs of steaming coffee in front of each of them, Dad settled into the captain's chair at the head of the table. He took a sip and looked directly at Sawyer. "Let's start at the beginning, shall we? Go ahead, son."

The fragrant muffin turned to sawdust in Sawyer's mouth, but he swallowed it anyway and washed it down with a slosh of coffee. Here went nothing. "Anna's pregnant with my baby."

Beside him, she sagged deeper into the chair and closed her eyes.

"I see." Dad's hands wrapped around his mug.

"We, uh, got together a few times in June around Trev's wedding. Then Anna disappeared and quit replying to my texts or calls." Sawyer took a deep breath. "Until today."

"What brought you back today?" Dad's voice remained steady as he looked at Anna.

When she didn't respond, Sawyer did. "She wants me to sign papers to release the baby for adoption."

Mom's hand flew to cover her mouth.

"Is there any question about who the father is?" Dad went on.

Sawyer's brain hadn't even gone there.

Anna straightened. This time her hostile glare arrowed straight at Dad. "No question at all."

Dad studied her for a long moment. He opened his mouth again, but Mom's hand came to rest on his forearm.

"When is the baby due?" Mom asked.

"Mid-March." Anna picked a chocolate chip off her muffin.

"I'd like her to stay until the new year, at the very least." Possibly forever. "Anna may not have office experience, but she understands computers and is a quick study, so I thought this would kill two birds with one stone, so to speak. I just... I just can't sign those papers spur of the moment. I need to think about the options and pray over them." The words felt foreign coming out of his mouth, but everything had changed since Ace's accident.

Dad nodded slowly. "It's never a good idea to make important decisions hastily. What do you think, Gloria? Is it worth giving Anna a shot at the job and see how she does?"

Say no.

Anna held her breath as she waited for Gloria Delgado's response. No matter what Sawyer told her about his parents' knowledge of his reputation, this had to be a bitter pill for his mother to swallow. She wouldn't be able to make nice with the wanton girl who'd enticed her precious son and gotten pregnant.

What *had* she been thinking back in June? Definitely not that God would nudge her conscience.

"Yes, I think we can give this arrangement a try." Gloria smiled across the table at Anna. "If you're sure about the apartment, I'll send Elnora out to clean it tomorrow. It's been vacant for a couple of years, so it needs a good scrubbing. You're welcome to our guest room for tonight." She gave Sawyer a look that said he'd better not take advantage of it.

As if Anna would let him. One last try. "Please. All this isn't necessary. I'll drive back to town and stay with Sabrina tonight." Then return to Bozeman to try to figure out what to do without Sawyer's signature. If only she hadn't tipped him off, she might have kept his name right out of it. Pretended she didn't know.

Too late.

The old Sawyer would have signed with barely a blink, wouldn't he? This new one was more serious. More focused. *Admit it, Anna. Also more attractive.* Nope. She wasn't admitting anything.

"Oh, no. Our road is treacherous after dark if you're not used to all the hairpin curves." Gloria shook her head. "We'd much rather you stayed."

"We'll be done inoculating this round of calves tomorrow, Dad." Sawyer leaned onto the table, looking past her at Russ. "Then maybe I can take the weekend to help Anna move over from Bozeman?"

Gloria clasped her hands together. "So she could start Monday, then? That would be lovely."

Lovely was not the word Anna was thinking of. "Really, Sawyer, you don't have to—"

He grinned at her, the smirk of someone who'd won the battle. "Sure. You need me. You shouldn't be lifting heavy boxes in your condition."

In her condition? She sputtered, glaring at him.

Sawyer had only won a battle, not the war. She couldn't let him, though he was going to smother her long before New Year's. "I don't need to bring that much. It's only for a couple of months. I can leave my apartment set up." Unless the garage apartment wasn't furnished? "I would need to give my thirty-day notice by the end of the month, which means it's mine until the end of November. There's no point to releasing it, since I'll need a place to live again a month later."

His eyes glimmered and his lips stayed curved in his steady smile. He wasn't buying the fact that he'd lose.

Anna needed to retreat. Study her hand. Her mind had only spun on the half hour drive up the mountain to the ranch. She'd been so sure she knew how he'd respond. She'd be in and out of Saddle Springs in no time and could nurse her damaged heart as she prepared to give away her baby. That would atone for her wrongdoing, wouldn't it?

Sawyer skewed everything. It sounded like he'd had an encounter with God as she had since summer. That should offer an easy road through this.

Too bad she couldn't just give in. Couldn't simply accept what he seemed to be offering, but that wasn't going to work. He thought he'd seen the game board, but he didn't know the cards in her discard pile. Cards that would change everything if he ever caught a glimpse. Cards she'd throw away all over again if she could.

Anna's trembling hands lifted the mug to her lips. Was Sawyer right? Should she be avoiding coffee? She took a small sip and set it back down.

Sawyer nudged her plate closer. "Eat your muffin. Our ranch cook, Ruthie, makes the best ones ever." Then he helped himself to a second one and slathered it with butter. The guy seemed to have regained his appetite, to say nothing of his bossiness.

She'd like to refuse, but her tummy grumbled in protest. Sawyer was right... again. Anna had a bite. The delectable flavor burst on her tongue, awakening all her taste buds. She could live with Ruthie's cooking, for sure.

"Would you like me to show you up to your room?" Gloria asked.

"I'll take her over to see the garage apartment first." Sawyer spoke before Anna could reply.

And she wanted to see it. But not tonight. Not with Sawyer.

"I assume you're giving her Trevor's old room for tonight," he said to Gloria. "I'll get her settled."

Anna didn't miss the pointed look his mom sent his way, and her cheeks flushed. As though she'd welcome Sawyer into her bedroom tonight, or ever again.

He popped the last of his muffin into his mouth. "Come on. Let's go have a look at the apartment, and we'll grab your overnight bag from your car on the way back."

Why did she keep arguing with this obstinate cowboy? It was like he never heard a word she said. Of course, he'd noticed her bag in the backseat and knew she hadn't left it at Sabrina's.

"Fine. Whatever you say." She rose as he pulled her chair away for her.

He leaned close and whispered, "I won't forget you said that."

This was going to be the longest ten weeks of her life, but somehow, she needed to stay strong. For the baby's sake. For her own.

And for Sawyer's.

Chapter 3

S awyer tried to keep the smug grin off his face as he pointed his black pickup toward Bozeman. He'd won another round. He'd talked Anna into leaving her car at the ranch, since the truck with its canopy could hold so much more.

"I don't know what you're trying to prove." Anna sat in the passenger seat, arms crossed over her belly.

"That I'm a responsible human being?" He kept his voice light.

She let out an unladylike snort. "That's new. And here I thought you were just going all alpha male on me."

Probably a bit of that, too. Being the youngest of three brothers hadn't made him a doormat. He'd learned to assert himself at a young age or get bowled over. Sawyer cringed. It was entirely possible he'd taken that too far.

He took a deep breath. Honesty was the best policy. Right? That's what his parents were forever trying to drill into his thick skull. "A few things have changed since... you and I met."

Her eyebrows hiked as she looked over at him, but she didn't respond.

"I was pretty full of myself."

Silence.

"What, you've got nothing to say to that?"

Anna shrugged. "We both were."

Unexpected. But, yes, true. "Winning an all-around champion trophy was everything to me, as you know. I'm not sure what I thought it would get me. More bragging rights, I suppose. Proof that Sawyer Delgado was a man worth reckoning with."

She nodded. Waited for more.

Sawyer tightened his hands on the steering wheel. "Then a buddy of mine was bucked off a bronc during competition." Maybe recounting the accident while he was driving was a bad idea.

"Doesn't that happen a lot?"

"Yes." He'd told her about the eight-second ride back in June. The way points were scored. "I've hit the dirt hundreds of times." He took a deep breath. "Ace was badly trampled in a freak accident. He's still in a coma a month later."

"Oh, no. That's terrible." Her words came as from a distance.

Sawyer hung onto the present with all his willpower. "Of course, that wasn't the first injury I've seen on the circuit. Broken bones and concussions are common. Had a few myself. But Ace's accident knocked some sense into me."

Anna studied his face.

"I realized I wasn't invincible. That death is only a failed heartbeat away. That eternity is real. That Eaglecrest is a beautiful place, and I have a family who loves me and needs me." He glanced across the cab at her. "And that I hadn't left a legacy of my own worth mentioning. Or, I thought I hadn't."

Her eyes narrowed.

Yep, the sensitive moment of understanding had passed. What had he thought, that he'd bare his heart and the switch would flip forever in his favor? She was going to make him work for his solution. And maybe that was good. They barely knew each other. Much of the time they'd been together had been spent in heated passion. Maybe, as they got to know each other without that in the way, they wouldn't even like what was left.

Once Sawyer would have disdained anyone his brothers or sisters-in-law thought was okay. But now he hung onto the fact that Trevor had tried to warn Anna of Sawyer's reputation, that Cheri and Denae liked her and thought of her as a friend.

The problem had been with Sawyer, not with Anna. And he'd turned over a new leaf. He was going to do the right thing for her and their baby, and it wouldn't be a hardship at all, because Anna was amazing. He was halfway in love with her already.

Easy, right?

Not that he'd ever shied away from the hard things.

And he wouldn't this time, either. This time, everything was at stake.

It had to be God's will for Sawyer to step up as a responsible adult and create a family for his child.

His child.

He was going to be a father.

ANNA HAD NEVER PACKED into pristine new cardboard boxes before. She was used to scrounging behind liquor stores and supermarkets, but Sawyer simply pulled into U-Haul and bought a bunch. To save time, he said.

She pointed him into the kitchen to pack food and dishes since the garage apartment did not come fully equipped. There was no way she'd take her meals with Sawyer and his parents. She'd spend far too much time with them all — especially Gloria — as it was.

Alone in her bedroom, Anna rested her hand on her slightly thickening belly. "I'm sorry, baby. This isn't working out like I thought it would, but you'll be okay, I promise. There's a perfect mommy out there for you."

And it wasn't her. She knew that, although sometimes it was hard to remember. Sawyer hadn't said anything, but she could tell what he was thinking. He thought there was a chance the three of them would be a family, but it wasn't that easy.

But, while she might not need to purchase any baby clothes or a crib or other equipment, she would need maternity clothes at some point. The button on her jeans was already getting uncomfortable, and she had five months of increasing girth to go.

What *had* she been thinking in June? How come she'd thought she could outsmart *him*? To say nothing of outrunning her mother. Outrunning genetics.

Anna shoved the thoughts aside for the millionth time and yanked open the top drawer in her dresser. Underwear, socks, and cozy pajamas tumbled into her open box. Second drawer. She scooped a stack of T-shirts into the box. When the dresser was empty, she moved to the closet. Should she pack her dresses into boxes, or drape them over boxes in the truck's backseat? She wouldn't even need most of them, since the ones that weren't summer sundresses were too fitted for her changing form. She pulled two long-sleeved dresses off their hangers and folded them into her box.

This was crazy. Anna sagged to the edge of the bed. She didn't want to move back to Saddle Springs for the next ten weeks, let alone to Eaglecrest. She didn't want to be pregnant. She wanted to rewind reality to the night she'd met Sawyer and make a different choice.

It wasn't like she hadn't seen him flirting with Tori Carmichael in the Branding Iron before she'd waited on the table that included their group of friends. Anna had watched Sawyer switch that charm from Tori to her in the blink of an eye. She'd also seen Tori's discomfort, but that wasn't why Anna had stepped up to the challenge. She had her own reasons that had nothing to do with Tori.

Sabrina had been excited to pass along the news that Tori and Garret had married in a small, private ceremony a few weeks ago. Anna hadn't been surprised. She was only surprised at how long it had taken. No, Tori had been no threat to her back in June.

In her mind's eye, Anna deflated the cocky rodeo star with a well-timed comeback and walked away. That's what a smart Anna would have done. Instead, the desperate, stupid Anna had come out to play. The one who'd somehow thought two wrongs could make a right. They couldn't. And now she was paying for it.

A small sound at the doorway caused her head to jerk in that direction. Sawyer filled the opening with his broad shoulders, his navy T-shirt tucked into worn jeans. Although he'd removed his Stetson, the large brass buckle on his belt announced his status as a rodeo cowboy, not some random guy who lived out west. As if he could ever be random.

But it was his dark, piercing eyes that caught at her heart as she stared back. They seemed to drill right into her soul and expose her very thoughts. She needed shields.

Anna managed a small smile. "How's it going?" She hadn't wanted his help — still didn't — but she appreciated it. Sort of.

The cords in his tanned arms rippled as he crossed them over his muscular chest. "Okay, but I'm getting hungry. Want me to order a pizza, or do you want a change of scenery? We can go out and grab a burger or something."

Pizza delivery reminded her of hot June nights. She pushed off the bed. "I've got some boxed mac-and-cheese. I'll fix that." If she could get through the doorway.

Sawyer shook his head. "You need a break, not more work. Plus, you need better nutrition to grow that baby. Scratch the pizza. Want a salad?"

She narrowed her gaze at him. "Pizza sounds good, actually."

He smirked. "With a side salad."

"Whatever." Anna glared at him. "I'll place the order."

"Extra pepperoni." He stepped back marginally, allowing her access to the small living area.

"I know what you like."

"Do you?" Sawyer was so close she could feel his breath on her cheek. "I've been thinking about that, and I'm not sure you do."

"Don't." Somehow her whisper sounded weak. Like she really meant to say the opposite.

"I like *you*." Sawyer's hands touched her arms, but she jerked away.

"Stop it. We agreed to act like adults over this."

"You agreed. I didn't. On the other hand, I'm feeling quite adult right now. I'm going to be a daddy."

Anna's gaze flew to meet his. "No, you're not. The baby will grow up in someone else's home. We might have created this life, but the titles of mom and dad will go to someone else."

"We didn't create this life, sweetheart."

She flinched at his tender tone, his term of endearment.

"God did. Yeah, He doesn't usually create life out of thin air, I'll grant you that. But He could definitely have prevented this pregnancy."

"Why didn't He, then?" Why, oh why?

Sawyer's fingers caressed her cheek. "Because He has a plan for all of us. For you. For me. For the little one."

Somehow Anna leaned into his touch for a brief second before regaining her senses and pulling away. "And for the couple who's been praying to adopt a baby."

His dark gaze intensified as his hand dropped. He opened his mouth to respond then closed it again. Finally he heaved a sigh. "Sit down, order the pizza, and stay there until it comes."

She glowered at him. "There's too much to do." But she did curl her legs beneath her on the corner of the sofa while she poked through the contacts on her cell and placed the order.

He stood over her, reaching for her phone until she added salad. Then he smiled, nodded, and stepped back. When she set the phone down, he sat across from her, elbows on his knees as he leaned toward her. "You need to eat better, sweetheart. You're growing a human life in there."

Her temper flared. "I know what I'm doing. And stop calling me sweetheart."

Sawyer studied her. "Then you won't mind if we drop off a couple of boxes from your cupboard to the food pantry on our way out of town. You won't need all that packaged junk food. Ruthie will take care of you."

She surged to her feet. "If you think I'm just going to sit back and let you boss me around for the next ten weeks, think again. I'm twenty-six years old, not a child, and I'm perfectly capable of making my own decisions and cooking my own meals. Stop meddling."

"I'm just thinking of your wellbeing. The wellbeing of our baby."

"Don't you get it, Sawyer Delgado? This is not *our* baby. This is *the* baby. Someone else's baby. The sooner you get that through your head, the better this will be for all of us." Anna placed her hand over her belly. "Especially for the child."

He rose slowly and loomed in front of her. "Don't *you* get it, Anna Winter? I'm not conceding any time soon. I have plans of my own." His large, calloused hands cradled her face. "Plans for all three of us."

And then he lowered his mouth to hers and kissed her.

She was starving, and it wasn't for pizza. She was hungry for this man and his persuasive lips. For him to sweep her off her feet and...

No. That's how this whole mess had started. Anna shoved at his chest. "Don't kiss me." Too bad her words came out breathy.

Sawyer smirked. "Is that what your brain wants or what your heart wants? Because I'm thinking there's a disconnect."

CHAPTER 4

Did you get any sleep?"

Anna had answered the door in baggy gray sweats. Before he'd left for the hotel last night, she'd pulled her hair into a low ponytail, but many of the blond strands now hung limp and free, framing her pale face. She stared at him from dark-rimmed eyes. "Not much."

"Me neither." Sawyer held up the paper takeout bag and cardboard drink carrier. "I brought breakfast."

Her eyes riveted on the drinks. "Coffee?"

"Yes, but I'm not sure if—"

She pulled one of the cups free and cradled it in her hands then raised her eyebrows at him. "Not sure if what?"

"If it's a good idea," he finished lamely. "Is caffeine okay for the baby?"

"It's fine. What else do you have?"

"I brought you a sausage and egg sandwich, but—"

"Come on in." She stepped aside, sniffing the coffee.

Sawyer entered the apartment. At least she hadn't argued about letting him in. He'd been prepared to use that coffee as bribery. Maybe that's all it was. Oh, and the minor fact she was stranded without him.

He stopped where the entry hallway opened to the living room. At least ten more boxes were stacked along the wall, and any signs of personality throughout the apartment had been obliterated, not that there'd been much. He turned to Anna, eyebrows raised. "No wonder you didn't sleep. I thought I told you to leave the rest for morning."

She unwrapped the sandwich, not looking at him as she took a large bite, chewed, and swallowed. "Thanks. I was starving."

"Anna?" He tapped his boot on the floor.

"What? I tried to sleep. My mind kept spinning." She glared at him. "So I packed. I thought you'd be happy we don't have to hang around Bozeman so long." Another bite went in.

Should he have brought two sandwiches for her? No. He'd get her something healthier. She needed vegetables, but who ate salad for breakfast? What constituted a healthy breakfast for a pregnant woman, anyway? He had no clue. Kade could fill him in. Sawyer had made himself scarce the past few years and hadn't been around much when Cheri had been pregnant with Donovan. Or when Kade's first wife had been expecting Jericho.

He needed a crash course in pregnancy.

But when Anna folded up her empty wrapper a minute later and eyed the second sandwich — his — he handed it over without a word.

"You ate already?" she asked around a mouthful.

The answer would be no. But there was a drive-through a block away, so he could get another easily. Looked like she hadn't been teasing about how hungry she was. 'Eating for two' appeared to be a real thing. Huh.

He took a seat, sipped his coffee, and ignored his rumbling gut while she inhaled the second sandwich. Then she curled up at the other end of the sofa with her cup.

Sawyer studied her. She seemed sated for the moment. "What's left to be done?"

"Not much." Anna glanced his way then leaned back, closing her eyes.

His gaze settled on her belly. Did his imagination deceive him, or was it slightly rounded? Maybe her sweats were bulkier in the waist than her jeans. Either way, her body would be filling out soon enough. His baby grew inside.

His baby. Not *the* baby, no matter what she claimed. A living soul that he'd participated in creating. A miracle, even though its conception was nothing to brag about. Somehow, God had been preparing Sawyer for this moment in life.

"What're you staring at?" Anna's voice sounded wary.

Sawyer's gaze flew to her face. None of the longing he felt was mirrored in her narrowed expression. What, had he expected she'd suddenly change her mind and fall into his arms? Might not have expected it, but hope sprang eternal. The kiss last night had reassured him she wasn't completely immune.

He wanted to hold her tight. Kiss her. Feel that tiny

bulge pressing against him. Feel it a little bigger the next day and the next and the next.

"Marry me, Anna."

Eyes blazing, she flew off the end of the sofa, the take-out cup arcing to the floor, coffee with a shot of cream spilling across the beige carpet.

Sawyer froze, gaze riveted to the spot, seeing Ace's blood spilled in the arena's dust.

"Look what you made me do." Anna stalked away and came back a moment later with a wad of paper towels. She knelt and began blotting up the liquid.

Coffee. It was only coffee. "I'm sorry. Here, let me." He crouched beside her and reached for the paper towel.

She pulled away. "You want to do something useful? Start hauling boxes out to the truck. The sooner we're out of here..."

The sooner they'd be stuck in the truck together for five hours. He raised his eyebrows at her.

Anna closed her eyes and took a deep breath, like she was trying to pull patience out of the depths of her being. Maybe she was.

He had ten weeks to win her over. It might take every minute of them. Sawyer rocked back on his heels and stood. "Your wish is my command."

Anna blew a strand of hair from her face. "Then sign the papers. They're on my bed. I'll be happy to unpack."

"Any wish but that one." He eyed her. "Nearly any."

"You talk big, cowboy," she muttered.

He always had. He'd been nothing but a bag of hot air, full of himself. He was different now, but she wasn't seeing it. Maybe her lenses were still colored from their past. Or maybe he was falling back into old patterns.

God? There's so much at stake here. Please help me.

Patience. Sawyer might be used to snap life-and-death decisions, but this situation was different.

"Anything left in your bedroom, or are all the boxes stacked out here?"

She settled back on her heels and looked up at him. "I moved most of them. If you go in there, you'll think I haven't packed, but I have. The clothes that are left are ones I won't be able to wear for much longer, anyway."

Sawyer remembered how ginormous Cheri had been before Donovan's birth. Yeah, Anna's normal wardrobe was not going to cut it. "So let's go to the mall."

She rolled her eyes. "Guys don't go maternity clothes shopping."

"Why not?"

"We're not a couple, remember? And there's no rush. Sabrina and I will drive down to Missoula sometime in the next few weeks, unless your mom won't give me a day off."

His mind raced. "This is part of your expenses that I promised to help with. Do you want to hit the mall on the way out of town, or go now then come back and load the truck?"

Anna sighed. "You don't give up, do you?"

She was starting to get the picture.

"I don't. About anything."

"My head hurts." Anna rubbed the tight band around her forehead. Stress, for sure. If only Sawyer would give her some space, but wherever she turned, he was there, watching her with a worried frown, taking a box from her, telling her to sit down. It was enough to drive a woman stark raving mad.

And he wasn't like anything she'd expected from the guy she knew in June.

He pulled his phone out of his pocket and tapped into it. A moment later he looked up. "Do you have anything with acetaminophen in it? Or I guess everything is packed away. You shouldn't have ibuprofen or acetylsalicylic acid."

Her temper flared. "Would you stop mothering me?"

"Not until you start mothering yourself." His gaze flicked to her midsection, and the unsaid words were clear. *Or until you start mothering the baby.*

She stomped over to her purse, unzipped it, and yanked out a small bottle. She gulped two pills dry and stuffed the bottle back inside. When she turned, Sawyer held out a bottle of water. She rolled her eyes but took a swallow.

The apartment seemed empty, even with her clothes in the closet and the lamps beside the sofa and big chair. She'd left her queen bed made, since the Eaglecrest apartment boasted a king. Thankfully, Gloria had scrounged up spare bedding that fit.

Walking out seemed so final, even though she'd be back at New Year's. Was she really doing the right thing, going with Sawyer? He was so pushy. *Marry me*, he'd said. If only he knew how much she wanted to do just that, he'd haul her down to the nearest courthouse on Monday morning, and they'd be wed within the hour.

And divorced within the year.

Meanwhile, he refused to sign the adoption agency's paperwork unless she went through with his cockamamie plan. It probably served her right for what she'd done. Even more so for what she'd intended. If this was to be her punishment, she'd endure it, even if it crushed her soul for the rest of her life. And it would.

Not only leaving Sawyer for the final time, but leaving their baby in the hands of strangers. She blinked back tears.

Be strong. It's best. For all of us.

Sawyer's arm circled her shoulders. "Hey, sweetheart."

She leaned into him as sobs broke free. "It's too hard."

He gathered her close, his cheek resting on the top of her head, his hands caressing her back. "What's too hard?"

"Everything." She should push away from this security. And she would. Soon.

"God's got it, Anna. He's got *us*."

"You didn't used to talk like that." The thing was, she'd come to believe in God herself. She'd found a measure of faith in the dark days as she grappled with the pregnancy.

"I know." Sawyer's hands slid down her arms as he pulled back enough to look at her. "You've met my family. You know how I was raised. Church every Sunday. Family devotions every morning at the breakfast table."

Anna tried to imagine what daily family devotions might be like. Failed.

He caught her hands. "I even led the youth group when I was in high school."

"I have a hard time picturing that." Although he certainly didn't lack the boldness for it.

Sawyer chuckled. "True story, though."

"What happened?"

"Got too big for my britches. I'd done pretty well with the town gymkhanas then local rodeos. Figured I was destined for bigger things than a ranch in the middle of nowhere, Montana."

"And then? What changed you?" Because, apparently, there was more to his story.

His fingers tightened around hers and he looked away, jaw tense. "My buddy Ace. Cramer was a solid bronc, got Ace stretched out horizontal. He hung on long enough to get the back of his head cracked a good one as the mustang's hindquarters bucked into the air."

Sawyer's voice came from a distant place. That place where his unfocused eyes stared. "Ace slid to the dirt but didn't roll away. Couldn't. He was likely already unconscious. And the horse's rear hooves collided with his head before the pickup rider could get in there."

"You watched it happen?" she asked softly.

"Yeah." His grip was so intense, his gaze so distant, it seemed like he was watching it again. "I thought I'd seen everything over the years. Kept waiting for him to roll out of the way, spring up, wave his hat at the crowd. He didn't."

"But he didn't die, from what you said." Small comfort, if any at all.

Sawyer's jaw twitched. "I was a blubbering mess, but God was there, waiting for me to turn back to Him. He'd been there all along, but I'd been blind. Willfully, stupidly, arrogantly blind."

"So you left the circuit? But you're so good at it."

His eyebrows peaked. "And how would you know?"

Heat shot up her face, and she pulled her hands away. "I might've watched you ride on TV." Seen a few interviews. Followed him online. Minor stuff. Okay, stalker stuff, but she'd felt the need.

"And you tell me you don't care about me?" Sawyer's tone seemed light, but the challenge in his dark eyes was real.

"Not exactly what I said." Anna stepped out of his reach. "We should get going. There's a long drive ahead of us."

"We're stopping at the mall for lunch and to find you some clothes."

Lunch, she needed. Fine, she also needed maternity clothes. Missoula might be a whole lot bigger than Bozeman, but the nearby mall had decent selections. It wasn't like these were garments destined to be forever favorites. After March, she'd never wear them again.

March. She just had to hang in there until she could hand the baby off to the caseworker. And she needed Sawyer's signature to do that.

Let him pay for her clothes.

CHAPTER 5

The return drive was long and quiet. Sawyer couldn't count the times he'd tried to start a conversation before he'd given up and cranked For King and Country on Spotify.

He'd winced over her lunch choices and handed over his credit card for half a dozen flowing tops, a pretty dress, flannel pajamas, and several pairs of leggings and jeans. He doubted she'd bought enough clothes, but her selections would see her through for a while.

Sawyer maneuvered the truck through Saddle Springs, across the bridge, and up the winding mountain road toward Eaglecrest while keeping an eye on Anna. She seemed to be asleep, leaning against the window, her hair veiling her features.

Both his brothers' trucks sat in front of his parents' garage, the first time they'd all be together since Anna had re-entered his life. Hopefully Cheri and Denae would welcome her.

He was over-thinking everything a thousand times over. *Please, God, be with us this evening. You know my heart.* His heart had found a lot to admire in Anna over the past few days. She was strong... but she was dead set on giving up the baby. Why had she practically fallen into a rage when he offered the obvious solution? Would marriage to him be that abhorrent?

She didn't stir when he parked the truck and turned off the ignition, so he reached over and touched her knee. "Anna? We're home."

"What?" She lurched upright and looked around. "Oh." Then her head tipped back against the headrest as she took a deep breath.

"You okay, sweetheart?"

"Don't sweetheart me." But her voice stayed flat.

He'd rather hear a little fire, but he wouldn't prod her for it. Not right now. "Ruthie's got dinner ready. I'll get Kade and Trev to help me haul your stuff up to the apartment after we've eaten, but you can stay in the house another night if you like. You don't have to..."

Anna shoved the truck door open and slid down.

All right then. "I'd have gotten that for you, you know."

Slam. She stood there in the angling sunshine, tugging her bulky sweater around her middle, looking so forlorn he itched to hold her close. That would bring out the fire, for sure.

Sawyer came around the truck and slung his arm over her shoulder. Of course, she shifted away. "Ready?"

"No." But she took a deep breath and started walking toward the house.

"No one's here to judge."

Anna didn't look back at him, so he hurried to catch up and open the door for her to enter.

"They're here!" yelled Harmony, running toward them then sliding in the last few feet.

Sawyer caught his niece before she bowled into Anna. "Hey, you. Looks like you missed me."

The eight-year-old gave him a tickly kiss on his bristly cheek. "Always, Uncle Sawyer." Then she smiled at his companion. "Hi, Miss Anna."

By then Jericho and Donovan had made their appearance. Sawyer scooped up the littlest Delgado and blew a raspberry on his tummy. The toddler giggled and squirmed.

"Hey, Anna. Welcome to Eaglecrest." Cheri moved in for a hug. "Good drive from Bozeman? The fall colors must have been beautiful."

They had been, but Sawyer doubted Anna had noticed.

Cheri winked at Sawyer and steered Anna toward the dining room. "You're just in time for dinner. Ruthie outdid herself today, so I hope you're hungry."

Anna murmured agreement, and Sawyer grinned. She was never *not* hungry. He hadn't had a clue how much a pregnant woman could pack away before the past few days. At least here he knew the meals would be well-rounded. He could trust Ruthie to know what Anna should eat to grow a healthy baby.

"Bro." Kade jabbed his shoulder. "How're things?"

Sawyer sighed. "Could be better." But they could also be worse. She was here, wasn't she? For ten weeks. Long enough for Sawyer to work his charm. If he couldn't bring her around in that time frame, he didn't deserve her.

There was something messed up in that way of thinking, but he didn't have time to figure it out. Not with the aromas of roast beef and sautéed green beans and other delectable foods drifting from the dining room.

"We're praying for you both."

Once Sawyer would have punched his brother for saying that. Not enough to knock him out, but enough to let him know the words weren't welcome. Things had changed for sure. "Thanks. We need it."

Kade eyed him then angled his head toward the dining room, where the voices of their family wafted back and forth. Denae's voice rose above the others. Harmony giggled. Donovan hollered his displeasure.

Why had he resisted family for so long? How could he have been so dazzled by danger, dalliance, and derring-do that he'd ignored the fact that love and acceptance and foundations were vastly more important?

Sawyer entered the dining room ahead of Kade and moved directly to Anna's side. Harmony had made place cards, adding a roly-poly drawing of each family member beside their names. She was a talented kid — no surprise since her mother was a sought-after mural artist. And she was smart enough to know that Sawyer's place was beside Anna.

He seated her next to Denae, with Kade and Cheri's motley crew along the other side of the long table and Dad and Mom seated at either end.

Dad cleared his throat and held out his hands to Sawyer

on one side and Jericho on the other. "Father in heaven, we are so thankful for Your many blessings."

Sawyer savored the feel of Anna's hand within his, even as he did his best to focus on his father's prayer.

"Thank You for giving Sawyer and Anna safety on the road this weekend. I pray that You will give them wisdom..."

Anna tried to pull away, but Sawyer didn't release her. He let his thumb smooth little circles on the side of her thumb and willed her to relax just a little. That didn't happen until Dad shifted to praying for Trevor and Denae then Kade and Cheri and finally brought his lengthy prayer to a close with gratefulness for the food before them.

Sawyer added a silent postscript of his own, asking God to show him what was holding Anna back. Asking Him to remove the barriers she'd placed to keep him at a distance.

Why? He needed to know. Needed to fix.

Correction. Needed to let *God* fix.

THIS COULD BE HER FAMILY. Her normal. Anna couldn't keep her gaze from landing on little Donovan across the table time and again. Just as often, she looked elsewhere quickly.

Stories around town rumored that Jericho wasn't Kade's, and Anna knew for a fact that Cheri's daughter, Harmony, wasn't Kade's, either. Donovan, on the other hand, carried Delgado features through and through.

Would her baby — no, *the* baby — have as much dark

hair as he did? Look as much like Sawyer as Donovan looked like Kade? She'd never know. The plan was to have the delivery-room nurse remove the newborn immediately, right into the arms of the new parents. It would be easier that way.

It wasn't going to be easy, no matter what. Once again, she pushed aside the self-recrimination. The only way out of this mess, the only way to prove to God she was serious, the only way to redeem herself, was to move forward with her revised plans. Not the originals.

She'd felt some peace before Sawyer bullied his way in to micromanage her life. Now she was more confused than ever.

"Have you done much riding?" Cheri met Anna's gaze from across the table.

"On a horse?"

Someone snickered. Better not have been Sawyer.

Cheri smiled. "Well, this *is* a ranch so, yes, that's what I meant. I'm taking the kids out for a ride along the river tomorrow afternoon since the weather is great, and I wondered if you'd like to come."

"I'm working."

"It's not safe," said Sawyer at the same time.

Anna pivoted in her seat to glare at him. "Just because your—"

His scowl stopped her. "It's not that. It's the trotting and bouncing. I looked it up, and horseback riding could be bad for the baby."

"I rode through my pregnancy with Donovan." Cheri hiked her eyebrows and looked between them. "It's fine. We have some placid horses around here — no one's talking about her riding Debonair or Bowen up in the canyons or racing barrels."

"I'd like to learn to ride." Anna stared into Sawyer's eyes as she said the words. Daring him.

"After the baby."

"I won't be here after the baby."

The scowl deepened. "No riding." He turned and looked at Cheri. "Promise me."

Cheri held up both hands in surrender. "It was only an idea."

Anna felt the eyes of everyone around the table taking in the confrontation, but she had to put a stop to him. They'd been back together — geographically — only a few days, and already she wanted to throttle him. She rose slowly. "Sawyer Delgado, you are not the boss of me. I am perfectly capable of making my own decisions." Right. That's how come she was stuck at Eaglecrest for the next ten weeks.

"Is she angry, Mommy?" She heard Jericho's curious voice over the pounding in her ears.

She wanted nothing more than to bolt outside, climb in her little car, and speed back to Bozeman. But, if she did that, she'd be stuck with raising this baby by herself. She needed Sawyer to sign those stupid papers, but did that mean she needed to submit to every whim and old-wives-tale he came up with?

Yes, she did.

Slowly, she sank back to her seat, still shooting fiery

darts with her eyes. Her hands trembled as she reached for her fork.

"Please pass the Yorkshire puddings," Trevor requested from beyond Denae.

A plate circled the other side of the table to him. Kade cut up scraps of the roast for Donovan. Gloria asked Denae about the novel she was currently editing. Once Anna had been fascinated that she knew a renowned professional romance editor. Now, she didn't want to know how Denae would analyze Sawyer's behavior, or worse, Anna's. Denae was notorious for plotting the relationships of those around her on some mythical romance graph.

Anna likely didn't fit on Denae's chart, anyway. Her friend edited for Christian and wholesome authors. They probably didn't write stories where foolish heroines got pregnant semi-purposefully and then tried to figure out their lives a little too late.

"Sorry," muttered Sawyer from beside her. "I didn't mean to make you angry."

Her temper flared again, but she forced it to subside before saying anything. "Then stop assuming you know what's best."

"I'll try."

Anna blinked. No way was she looking at him, even though he sounded contrite. "Good."

Trevor and Kade began discussing a week-long cattle roundup.

Her ears perked up. Surely Sawyer would go, too. It sounded like their hired hands would ride out with them, leaving Russ to manage the base ranch chores in their absence.

"What do you think, Sawyer?" asked Kade.

Anna stilled, staring at her plate, but she felt Sawyer's quick glance.

"You guys are used to doing the roundup without me, and I'm needed here."

What? No way. Just when she'd been fantasizing that she'd be free of him for ten percent of the remaining weeks.

"Dad's got everything covered at home," put in Trevor. "He's done it the past five years."

Everyone turned to stare at Sawyer.

"Stop hovering," she growled.

He took a deep breath. "At home, sure. But Dad isn't needed to take Anna for her checkup at the clinic."

Well, that was definitely true. And she did need to see a doctor at some point, probably. She'd avoided it so far other than the confirmation visit a couple of months back. "Neither are you." Anna glared at Sawyer. "You're not coming into the doctor's office with me."

"Well, uh..." His face flushed.

"Do you have an appointment yet?" asked Gloria. "I usually need to run into town once or twice a week, so I'm sure I can work around that."

"I have a car. I can drive myself."

"True enough." Gloria smiled. "Totally up to you, but if you want to save a little fuel, let me know. We generally try to bunch up appointments and errands so someone isn't driving in every day."

"Thank you." She wanted Sawyer's mother hovering in

the waiting room very little more than she wanted Sawyer himself. "I'll keep that in mind. The point is, there's no need for Sawyer to stay home from the roundup on my account. I don't need anything from him."

Other than his signature on the adoption papers.

"She's got you there," commented Trevor.

Yes!

Sawyer glared past Anna at his oldest brother then turned to Russ. "Dad?"

Russ chuckled. "Sounds to me like a week apart might do the both of you good. Give her a chance to breathe a little, son. And your brothers could sure use another experienced rider back in the deep valleys. We'll be getting snow up there soon."

"Okay, fine. I'll go." Sawyer shot her a look.

Likely a warning that he'd leave her with a ten-page list of instructions that she would ignore. For the first time this week, things were looking up.

CHAPTER 6

Ever heard of letting God handle things?"

Ignoring Kade, Sawyer shoved another log into the fire.

"He's lost the habit of it," commented Trevor.

Beyond the blaze, the two hired hands circled the fifty-some cow-calf pairs they'd rounded up so far. The cattle's breath hung like fog in the meadow, punctuated with occasional lowing. Temperatures this moonless night promised to plummet below zero, but Sawyer's big brothers seemed intent on keeping his temper simmering.

"I keep asking Him to handle Anna, but He seems in no hurry to do so."

"Patience has never been one of your virtues." Trevor poured water from the canteen into the old tin percolator they'd hauled on more cookouts than Sawyer could remember then dumped grounds into the basket.

"There's a limited amount of time here." Sawyer glowered at his brother.

"Not as limited as you're making it out to be," put in Kade. "There's still a couple of months left to this year, and then still more time before the baby's born."

"If I sign those stupid papers, the rest of her pregnancy might as well not exist. She'll be gone so quick I'll have whiplash. I'll have no say in anything."

"The thing is, you don't have a say now."

Sawyer stared at Kade in the flickering firelight. "Who asked you?"

"Dude. We're on your side." Trevor propped the perc on a rock beside the flames.

"You've got a funny way of showing it."

"There are options. You could raise the baby yourself."

Sawyer snorted. "I'm no Saint Kade, you know. Just because our perfect middle brother chose that route with Jer doesn't mean it's a good choice for me."

"If it's that or let your flesh-and-blood disappear into the state system? I'd think it was a viable option." Trevor settled on a stump across the fire.

"A private adoption isn't the same thing as the state system," Kade interjected mildly. "For the record. Anna would have the option of choosing the parents."

"Is that supposed to help?" Sawyer glared at his brothers.

Kade shrugged. "Setting the point straight. Daniela and I talked about that sort of thing a lot when she was carrying Jericho, but I'd already made up my mind."

Sawyer couldn't begin to imagine his life with a newborn and no wife. He'd managed to avoid Eaglecrest a lot while Kade was in that position with Jer. Thing was,

Jericho wasn't even Kade's child, but his brother had still taken the infant on.

"I wouldn't recommend the choice," Kade said. "It was brutal. I got no sleep and packed that kid everywhere with me for two years. Mom and Dad helped when they could, for sure, but he was totally my responsibility."

"You don't think I could handle that?"

Kade rolled his eyes. "If you thought that might be a viable option, you'd have already gone there, at least in your head. How many choices do you think you have?"

Two. Win or lose... and he wasn't going to lose. Losing meant Anna disappearing for good. Losing meant their baby belonging to someone else. Losing meant a shattered life with no meaning.

Huh. Wasn't that long ago his life revolved around winning the next event. Around shooting for that elusive all-around championship trophy. Around one buckle bunny after another. Now, suddenly, his life had no meaning without Anna and the baby in it?

No meaning without God.

He kept forgetting that. Kept getting trapped in ruts of his own making and ignoring his Maker and Redeemer.

Sawyer picked up a twig and snapped it into a dozen pieces, tossing each into the flames. His brother asked a valid question. What were his options? "I don't know."

Trevor turned the percolator with a long stick as coffee began to bubble. "Don't know what?"

"What the choices are. Besides the obvious."

"What are you trying to prove, making her stay here until New Year's?"

Wasn't it plain as the nose on his face? "I want her to agree to stay forever and marry me so we can raise our child together."

Kade let out a low whistle. "Told you, Trev."

"Still don't believe it," muttered Trevor.

"What? Is it so unfathomable that I'd want to do the right thing? Told you dumb cowboys that God clunked me upside the head. Just because I keep forgetting doesn't make it a lie."

"You were riding in Amarillo the night of Ace Desjardins' accident. You came home two days later." Kade eyed him. "I might be just a dumb cowboy, but it doesn't take a genius to figure out that had something to do with you quitting the circuit."

A chill having nothing to do with the freezing Montana night settled over Sawyer. "I don't want to talk about it."

"I think you need to." There was a brief silence, only broken by the creak of saddle leather from over in the meadow. "We saw the accident on TV, bro. On repeat and in slo-mo. It looked bad."

"It *was* bad." Sawyer heard the bleakness in his own voice. "Do you know that just a few days earlier, Ace's ex-girlfriend met up with the team in Abilene to tell him she was pregnant?"

"No way."

"News didn't report that," commented Kade.

"They didn't know. She'd done it on purpose, and now she wanted money to keep quiet about some of his less than savory activities." A lot of money. Ace had done well in rodeo. He was loaded.

"A baby trap." Trevor shook his head. "Denae told me about that as a plot device. Who knew it happened in real life?"

The joys of having a romance editor in the family. Sawyer shook his head. "Ace has been in a coma for a month now. What incentive does he have to regain consciousness? He's lost everything. His career. His reputation. Even his child. There's nothing left."

"There's God." Kade eyed the coffee bubbling through the percolator's glass bulb.

Thankfully, Ace had refound his faith not long before. The three of them— Sawyer, Ace, and Adam — had managed to keep God out of most everything they'd done for most of a decade. What kind of friend had he been? The other guys hadn't had nearly the spiritual grounding Sawyer'd had. He should have been a better example. A better friend.

If only he could do those years over again... but if he'd been following God's will, would he ever have left Eaglecrest and joined the rodeo circuit? Trying to make fresh decisions for his seventeen-year-old self was impossible. Better to save his brain cells for coming up with valid choices for his present self.

"I'm sorry about your friend, bro," Trevor said quietly. "But if it knocked some sense into your thick skull, I'm thanking God for it every day."

"While praying for Ace," added Kade.

"Yeah. Of course."

Sawyer swallowed hard, his throat thick with emotion. Growing up in the shadow of these two louts had been sheer torture, but maybe they weren't so bad. Maybe now they could be friends of sorts. Seemed Trevor and Kade had already found their way there.

He tossed a twig into the fire. "I messed up so bad. This thing with Anna… it's just a sample, but a really important one. I know God's forgiven me, but the consequences remain. I just don't know what to do."

"So, options." Trevor dug three thermal mugs out of the saddlebags. "There's got to be other alternatives besides your way or the highway. Let's not completely dismiss you raising the baby yourself. Keep all options open for now, no matter how weird the suggestion." He poured the coffee and handed out the mugs.

"An open adoption?" suggested Kade. "Someone you know, where you could see the baby grow up."

Sawyer snorted. "Like who, dude? You?"

"Maybe. I could talk to Cheri."

"That's the dumbest idea I've ever heard."

"Thought we'd agreed to keep judgment off the table for this phase," Trevor said mildly.

"That was before Kade tried to get his hands on my kid."

"Would that really be worse than never seeing him or her again?"

"Yeah." Sawyer glared between his brothers and watched them exchange a glance. "You're not taking me seriously here. I'm desperate."

"If you don't want suggestions, maybe it's prayer meeting time." Kade leaned forward, elbows on his knees, then tipped his Stetson off his head. "Lord, we've got a problem."

Praying with his brothers ought to be more comforting than this.

ANNA PULLED open the door to Shear Inspirations and stepped inside, sliding her sunglasses to the top of her head as her eyes adjusted.

The hair salon's middle-aged owner glanced over from blow-drying a customer's hair. "Well, if it isn't Anna Winter!" Then her gaze slid down Anna's length with a knowing smirk.

News traveled quickly in small towns like Saddle Springs, at least where Dora Yanovich was concerned. "Hi, Mrs. Yanovich. Is Sabrina working today?"

Dora glanced at the clock. "She's on break, but she has a nail job at three. I think she's gone over to Java Springs."

Forty-five minutes. Long enough for a quick catch-up. "Thanks." She reached for the door.

"I hear you're staying out at Eaglecrest Ranch with Sawyer Delgado. Never thought Russ and Gloria would stand for that sort of thing."

Anna sucked in a sharp breath and turned back slowly. "I'm staying in the apartment above the garage, which is *not* the same thing as living with Sawyer. I work in the ranch office."

"Convenient, though, isn't it?"

It was judgmental, gossiping women like Dora who'd

kept Anna averse to Christianity for so long. "It's a job."
Anna pushed out through the glass door at Dora's chuckle.
If that woman wasn't her friend Lauren's mother, she'd give
her a piece of her mind. Someone needed to. Not that it
would make a difference, most likely.

Anna glanced both ways and crossed the street to the
coffee shop. Several tables were surrounded by groups of
friends laughing and chatting with each other. A couple of
teen girls sat hunched over their phones on one of the sofas
by the fireplace, while another curled up with a paperback
in a big leather chair.

Sabrina turned from a tall stool at the counter and
waved. "Girl! Come have a coffee. Tell me everything."

"And a muffin." The shop's owner, Abigail Evening,
smiled at Anna from beyond Sabrina. Abigail was a breath
of fresh air after Dora. Even better, she was a breath of
pumpkin-spice filled air.

"Yes, please." Anna slid onto the stool next to Sabrina.
"I'll have a pumpkin-spice latte, and two gingerbread
cookies to go with it."

"Coming right up." Abigail turned into the hub of her
kitchen.

"Had your doctor's appointment?" asked Sabrina, more
quietly.

Anna sighed. "Yeah."

"Everything okay?"

"Hunky dory."

"Well, that's good, right? You want a healthy baby."

She didn't want a baby at all. "I'm supposed to have an

ultrasound next week." She blinked back tears. Oh, those stupid hormones.

"Your second one?"

Anna shook her head. "I managed to avoid it last time."

Her friend's perfectly manicured fingertips rested on her arm. "Sweetie, you have to face up to it."

"I don't want to see. I don't want to know the gender." Her voice quivered. "I don't want it to be real."

Abigail set Anna's latte and cookies in front of her with a motherly smile then turned to help another customer.

Anna wrapped her hands around the mug. At least Sawyer wasn't here to insist on decaf. Or wonder how many carbs were in the cookies.

"News for you, friend. It's real whether you want to face it or not." Sabrina hesitated. "Sawyer's going to want to come to your appointment."

"No way I'm letting him."

"It's his baby, too."

"It's not our baby. He or she will belong to someone else."

"It doesn't have to be that way."

"Don't go there. You're starting to sound like Sawyer."

Sabrina shrugged. "Maybe we're both right. Wasn't this what you wanted, back in June?"

"Not exactly." But too close.

"You wanted to get pregnant. You succeeded. Congratulations."

"Shh!" But no one was close enough to hear her friend's low voice.

"I hadn't counted on finding Jesus." That's what had

messed everything up. Not she regretted the love and sense of security she'd found in Him, but she could live without the overwhelming weight of conscience.

"See, I don't get that. Isn't being a Christian all about *letting go and letting God* or some inane platitude like that? I'm not seeing any letting go. You've got an agenda, and you're pursuing it like a horse with a burr under its saddle."

Tears filled Anna's eyes. "I thought I could count on you."

"To give you the advice you think you want? To stand by you and your dumb decision? Why, because you don't want to listen to the advice from your Christian friends?"

"I don't need this."

"Look, Anna. I'm sorry. I'm not trying to hurt you. But I don't understand, and I think I'd be a lousy friend if I were only an agreeable bobblehead. I care about you." She reached over and tapped Anna's midsection. "I care about what happens to your little one, as well."

So did Anna. Oh, she was definitely trying not to care, but it was getting harder and harder the longer things went. She'd had to attach the button extender on her jeans this morning for the first time.

Things were getting real.

Once she saw the images on the sonogram and felt the baby begin to move, her life of denial would be over.

It would be over even faster if Sawyer had his way.

Chapter 7

Sawyer circled Debonair around the tail end of the straggling herd. At best count, their small crew had rounded up all but a couple of the cow-calf pairs that had been turned out to the range last spring. A few additional calves were missing, likely taken out of action by a prowling mountain lion or maybe a grizzly bear. One of the hands had stayed upcountry to search for another day or two.

He was dusty and saddle-sore. A week of sleeping rolled up beside a dwindling fire and riding all daylight hours had about done him in. Food, a shower, and a soft bed were calling him.

And Anna.

She'd edged her way into his thoughts a thousand times a day. He'd summited a mountaintop at sunrise on Debonair and wished he could share the exquisite beauty with her. He'd surprised a pair of tumbling bear cubs and backed away, keeping a watchful eye for their mama, and wished Anna had the same fierce protectiveness toward their child. He'd watched a flock of Canada geese winging south in formation and, for once, didn't feel the itch to escape winter in southern climes. Not with Anna here in Montana.

Up ahead, his parents and sisters-in-law offered backup as the herd streamed through the gate and into their winter pasture. Mom kneed Friday into action, cutting off a calf balking at the unknown, while Dad circled Dazzle around the edge to help bring in the rear. Harmony and Jericho had climbed up on the log fence to watch, safely out of the way.

No Anna.

Had he really expected her to be out with the family, welcoming them in? Welcoming him?

In his dreams. It definitely happened in his dreams.

He and Kade pushed the last cow-calf pair through the gate. Kade swung it shut with a clang and turned for a high-five. "Good job, bro."

"You, too." Yeah, Kade and Trevor had been as exasperating all week as only brothers could be, but they were mostly all right. Cowboys Sawyer could be proud to ride with. They'd had some good talks, too.

Mom reined in beside them, watching the milling cattle. "They look fat and sassy."

"Sassy is definitely one word for them." Sawyer grunted.

Kade chuckled as he stretched both hands overhead, but his gaze was on his wife riding toward them. "They're in good shape... which is more than I can say for my soft kid brother here. You've been coddling the boy too much, Mom, but we'll make a man out of him yet."

Sawyer rolled his eyes, and the words rolled off his back with the motion. Once he'd have punched Kade for that, but it was just his brother's way of showing affection. "Whatever. Just because you old dudes can't keep up..."

Kade's laugh lifted above the melee as he swung off Bowen then plucked Cheri off her mare. They stood in the midst of the dust in the cold wind, locked in each other's arms, kissing like there was no tomorrow.

Sawyer tore his gaze back to his mother. "Where's Anna?"

"In town, but she should be back soon. She had a doctor's appointment today."

An appointment he'd badly wanted to go to. In fact, everything about Anna screamed desperation at him. He might have flirted with her in June partly to annoy his brothers, but she'd become more to him. Much, much more, especially since she'd walked back into his life little more than a week ago. She was strong. Beautiful. Feisty. And he wanted her to be his.

"We'll let the cattle settle for the night and run them through the gamut tomorrow. Meanwhile, Ruthie's got a big spread on, and I imagine you'd like a date with your pillow."

Sawyer pushed his dusty Stetson back on his head and nodded. "Sounds good. I'm mighty tired of Trevor's cooking. Beans and jerky can only take a man so far."

Mom laughed. "I promise there are no beans on the table tonight. Ruthie knows better."

Kade and Cheri ambled past, arms around each other's waists, both horses trailing behind them on loose reins. On the other side of the corral, Trevor and Denae were wrapped in a tight embrace.

Seemed like there was no place to look that didn't remind him the woman of his dreams wanted nothing to do with him. Would she still be that woman if she weren't carrying his baby? He suspected yes.

ANNA LEANED on the roof of her car and watched as Denae and Trevor strolled toward the ranch house arm in arm. Cheri, Kade, and their two older kids stood by the open stable doors, chatting with one of the cowhands as they handed off the reins to their horses. By the noisy, milling cattle in the pasture beyond the barn, the roundup was complete. That meant Sawyer was here somewhere.

She was only looking for him so she could avoid him.

There he was, dismounting from Debonair by the stable door. He placed his hands along the horse's nose, and Deb leaned into the touch. Horse and rider stood for a long moment, creating a tender picture Anna would remember forever.

"Hey, Anna." Denae dragged Trevor to a stop near the car. "How was your appointment? You saw Dr. Miller, right?"

"I did. It's all good."

"That's great. Ruthie's got a feast ready to welcome back the guys from the cattle drive. Coming over?"

If only she could retreat to the little apartment over the garage, but that was a surefire way to have Sawyer taking the steps two at a time to check on her. She didn't need him in her space; that was for sure. She'd never get rid of him.

"Yeah, I'll just take my groceries upstairs and be right over."

"Good." Denae grinned and turned back to Trevor. Both she and Cheri had done their best to set Anna at ease this past week. They'd been friendly before Sawyer — not bosom buddies, but close enough to stop and chat in the produce aisle at Manahan's Grocery or grab a coffee at Java Springs if they met on the street. Close enough Anna enjoyed serving their table and lingering there when they came into the Branding Iron for dinner. Close enough she'd scored an invitation to Denae and Trevor's wedding.

Look where that had gotten her.

Anna opened her trunk to retrieve her grocery bags, glancing toward where she'd last seen Sawyer, but he wasn't in sight. He'd certainly have something to say about the bags of salt-and-vinegar chips, packages of gingersnaps, and cartons of tutti-frutti ice cream. The cravings were real.

She grabbed all the handles in one go and managed to get the trunk slammed with her elbow before pivoting and slamming straight into a solid, broad chest that smelled of sweat and cows. Not a bad combination, all in all. Except now.

"Hey, let me get those."

"No, it's okay. I've got them." But she may as well be talking to a stone wall, since Sawyer simply plucked the bags out of her hands and turned toward the door that led up to the apartment. Exasperating man.

She dodged past him to block his way. "I said, I'll take them up."

His dark eyes burned into hers. "You don't have to buy food, you know. Just put it on Ruthie's list."

"I'm hungry all the time." It wasn't a lie.

A glimmer of a smile ghosted his mouth. "Like father, like son."

A baby boy like Sawyer? The words felt like a sucker punch. She could feel herself staring at him like a deer caught in the headlights.

His grin faded. "You okay?"

Not even a little bit. "I'm fine. Just give me the bags."

Sawyer leaned a little closer. "Sweetheart, here's the thing you keep forgetting. I can out-stubborn you."

"Don't sweet—"

But he managed to get his fingers around the knob and let himself in. He tromped up the stairs, bundles of fat grocery bags dangling on each side.

He looked mighty fine, and she could indulge her eyes for a few seconds. His well-fitting faded jeans were splotched with dried mud, his shearling-lined jean jacket had a smudge of dust — or something — on his right shoulder. Dirt even clung to his cowboy hat.

Ranching was no sissy job. The man had been up in the high country for a week, riding all day and probably half the night from the tales she'd heard about flushing calves out of thickets and keeping the herd together through the long hours of darkness. Sawyer was cowboy through and through.

He'd summited the wooden staircase and turned to look at her, still at the bottom. A smirk appeared and his dark eyes glimmered. "Enjoy the view?"

Far too much. "What view?"

His chuckle had an indulgent edge to it. Instead of setting the bags on the table at the head of the stairs, he turned into the space.

It wasn't like Anna could wait at the bottom while he put her groceries away and came down. Not when she didn't want him to analyze her choices, so she jogged up the stairs. "I've got it from here. Thanks."

Sawyer stood on the other side of the tiny island separating the kitchen from the dining space and lifted a carton of ice cream from the bag. "Tutti-frutti? Seriously?" His eyebrows shot into the shadows of his cowboy hat as he dug deeper into the bag. "Four of them?"

Anna wrapped her arms around her middle, but she couldn't reach as far as last week. "I get hungry at night."

"This." Sawyer held up a carton. "This is garbage. You're hungry? Eat some vegetables or protein or something." He peered into the next bag. Then the next, his expression only growing more pained with each revelation. "Anna."

"Don't Anna me. You're not the one who's pregnant. You don't get to tell me what to eat when. You have no idea what it's like. None."

"I'd like to know." Sawyer's voice was low.

"Sure, you would. Isn't it enough you're holding me

captive way up here at the end of the road? Now you have to interfere with every minute of my day?"

"You're hardly my captive. I've been gone for a week. You apparently have the ability to drive to Saddle Springs and go shopping. You have the means to drive away from Eaglecrest and never return."

"Not without the signed papers."

He shrugged one lean shoulder. "That's your choice, not mine. You consider that signature of vital importance, and I don't."

"Liar."

"Pardon me?" Those deep dark eyes bored into her soul.

But realization had kicked in. "If it didn't matter to you, you'd think nothing of signing and letting me be on my way."

"Bingo." His thumb and forefinger formed a circle. "You've got it in one. We're at cross-purposes, but make no mistake. You're not a hostage here. There's no lock and key, only free will."

It was her turn for eyebrows to climb. "That's the oddest definition of free will I've ever heard. You're pushing me. Crowding me. Giving me no out but the one you want." Like those cows herded into the pasture.

Sawyer's gaze never wavered. "Or you can outlast me."

"I will. Don't worry about that." She circled the island and hip-checked him over far enough that she could grab the ice cream and toss it into the freezer drawer of the stainless-steel refrigerator.

"Anna?" His voice had gentled.

She froze, her back to him, then straightened slowly and turned. "What?"

"Why am I like the plague to you? I get that I took advantage of you, but you were a willing party. I care about you, I care about the baby we created, and I want to take care of you both. Why is that the worst solution you could possibly imagine?"

Sawyer's hands hung at his sides, fists clenching and unclenching. If she took one step — that's all it would take, only one — in his direction, he'd hold her close. She'd be kissed. Treasured. Secure.

Until the truth came out.

She was under no illusions. The truth always had a way of revealing itself sooner or later, but it would be far better if it didn't surface until she was back in Bozeman. It was better if it were clearly evident that she had not followed through on her original intent.

Falling for Sawyer Delgado had not been part of that plan. Growing a conscience, stunted as it might be, and glimpsing God's love and grace had not been, either.

Anna was stuck between a rock and a hard place, a place where the events she'd set in motion before meeting Jesus made it impossible to follow Him completely.

No wonder her prayers were not being answered.

CHAPTER 8

This was killing Sawyer, piece by piece by piece. The father of an unborn child shouldn't be denied access to the doctor's office. According to his research, an ultrasound at this stage might reveal the baby's gender. How could Anna not want to know? Or was that just a bluff so he wouldn't beg for the information?

So he sat in his truck behind her little white car in front of the medical clinic, waiting.

Sawyer was lousy at waiting. His motto was simpler. *Make a plan. Execute it. Move on.* He tapped his fingers on the steering wheel to the beat of the music on his Spotify app. One song from For King and Country segued into the next, and the singers belted out a call for compromised women to realize they were more than what they saw in the mirror.

His heart cringed. He'd been that man. The one who'd taken advantage of women so many times it was a miracle only one carried his child. He hadn't been the kind of guy he'd want his daughter to go out with.

She'd be priceless, just like the song said. Just like her mama.

Sawyer closed his eyes. "Oh, Lord, what did I do?"

Trust Me.

Easy for God to say. He wasn't here in the trenches, trying to figure out how to atone for the mistakes of His past. How could Jesus possibly understand? He'd been sinless. Hadn't gotten Himself into a mess like Sawyer had.

The song wasn't only for women. It also challenged men to start again, giving honor until the end. An about face. Repentance.

"I'm sorry, Lord. I really, truly am. I want to do the right thing, start over, and give Anna the honor she deserves. Please let her accept that from me. I can't bear to think of the alternatives."

The door to the clinic opened, and a couple emerged.

Sawyer blinked. A couple? That was Anna and... whom? No. Stinkin'. Way. Dillon Scarborough?

Anna strode ahead of the man toward her car. She popped into the driver's seat and tried to slam the door, but Dillon blocked it, leaning in.

That was all Sawyer needed to see. In one second flat he was out of his truck and had Scarborough by the collar of his jacket. "What's going on here?"

Dillon turned to look at him, all blank innocence. "What do you mean? Just talking to my... friend here. Got a problem with that?"

"I think the lady has a problem with that." Sawyer stared at Anna's wan face. "Is the scum bothering you, sweetheart?"

That got a second's worth of fire in her eyes but then the flame extinguished. Only tiredness remained. "Everything's fine, Sawyer. Leave it."

Odd answer. Sawyer refocused on Dillon. He couldn't think of anyone he despised more than the vermin who'd come between Kade and Cheri years back and fathered Cheri's daughter, Harmony, in the process. "Move along, Scarborough."

"You heard the lady." Dillon stared back. "She's fine with my presence here. We were just talking."

"Are you looking to get punched out?" Sawyer kept his voice casual. "I can't tell you how happy that would make me. Comforting, even." There wasn't a remote chance Scarborough could take him on and win. He'd moved to Missoula a few years back, all but abandoning his so-called rights to visitation with Harmony. He'd also abandoned any semblance of fitness.

Dillon rolled his eyes. "The Delgado way. Violence."

"Better than the sleazy Scarborough way." Sawyer let go of the guy's collar but didn't give up an inch of bravado. He had a couple of inches on Scarborough. The other guy might outweigh him, but it was all flab. "Get out."

"Only because I was leaving anyway." Dillon adjusted his lapel. "Talk to you later, Anna. I'll give you a call."

She said nothing, and that sent all kinds of warnings roiling in Sawyer's gut.

Dillon smirked at Sawyer and strolled across the street. He did not get hit by a stray eighteen-wheeler, no matter how much Sawyer begged God in that moment.

Anna's car door slammed and locked. She yanked her

seatbelt across her body before turning the key in the starter.

He tapped on her window. "Hey, we need to talk."

She shook her head and slipped the transmission in gear.

What were his options? Throw himself on the hood like they did in movies? He refused to look like a desperate man with Scarborough across the street watching and laughing.

Anna applied her foot to the accelerator and peeled away from the curb.

Sawyer forced himself to walk, not run, back to his truck, and start after her, avoiding the sight of Scarborough's smug face. He followed her through town and over the bridge before drawing in a complete breath. There was no place she could lose him between here and Eaglecrest. She wasn't running from him. Not exactly. He still had a chance.

A chance for what?

He gripped the steering wheel as he kept the little white car in his sights on the tight turns.

Dillon Scarborough.

That had to be about the last person he'd expected to run into with Anna. Hadn't the idiot left Saddle Springs before Anna had moved here? She'd started waitressing at the Branding Iron the spring Kade had married Cheri. Less than three years back now.

She'd never really told him why she'd chosen Saddle Springs. He'd gotten the impression she'd moved here for the job, but wasn't that a bit odd? It wasn't like waitressing paid so well that it was worth uprooting for. She didn't seem to have family.

Sawyer didn't know anything about her background, come to think of it. Back in June, they'd been too... ah... busy. And since then, he hadn't really thought of it. Not that they'd spent much time just chatting lately. Still, Anna's history had gaps in it wide enough to run a herd of cattle through.

Scarborough's possessive posture grated on every last one of Sawyer's nerves. Were they together?

And even worse, was the baby she carried Sawyer's... or Dillon's?

THE BIG BLACK truck filled Anna's rearview mirror the whole way up the mountain road. Sawyer was angry. Not only that, he had questions... and he'd demand answers.

Why had Dillon chosen to drive up from Missoula today? He'd come to visit his parents, he'd said. But in reality, he'd come to check up on her.

She'd changed her mind so many times on what to do and how to handle things, and this past week had only made things worse. Sawyer had not played the part she'd expected of him.

Had she really thought he'd scrawl his signature on the bottom of that long legal document? A man from a tight-knit family like his would take a baby seriously, even a man who'd walked away from his moral upbringing. She'd made a snap judgment call and lost.

Wouldn't it be a fine sight to watch Sawyer punch Dillon's lights out, though? She couldn't let that happen, because Dillon would retaliate. He hated everything to do with the Delgados. He'd make sure Sawyer would eventually suffer for choosing her.

Because Sawyer had chosen. Everything in his stance, everything in his manner, everything in his eyes when he looked at her, told her his choice had been made. And while that was gratifying, it was also dangerous, because once he knew everything about her, he'd push her away.

By the expression on his face when she'd driven off, he wouldn't give up until he got to the bottom. She had to stall. Had to divert his attention, but how?

God would be no help. She'd messed up too much for that. She was on her own, and she'd been doing a lousy job so far.

Anna had no illuminating insights before she parked her car in front of the garage apartment door. No surprise that Sawyer's truck parked immediately behind her, blocking her in.

She exited the car as he jumped out of the truck, and he followed her into the tiny entry and up the steps. She rounded the dividing island and turned to face him.

"Talk to me." Sawyer stood at the top of the staircase, feet apart, arms crossed, eyes unyielding.

"I'm not sure what you want me to say." Oh, that was feeble.

"How long have you known Dillon Scarborough? And why was he invited to your ultrasound, and I was not?"

"He wasn't invited. He was waiting when I came out."

Anna didn't miss the flicker of relief that rippled across Sawyer's face.

"Then back to the first question."

All her life? "Quite a while."

"Where did you meet?"

She closed her eyes for a few seconds. "Sawyer, just leave it. It's not what you think."

"How do you know what I think?"

"It's obvious." Jealousy was oozing out of his very pores.

Sawyer stalked closer, his riveting gaze all that held Anna up. "It's because of him you moved to Saddle Springs. Because otherwise, it's just too much coincidence."

Too much truth there. She licked her lips, but no words came out.

"Do you know that Scarborough has always hated my family?"

"Oh, really?" Wow, that hadn't sounded confident at all.

"He has. As a teenager, he became so jealous of my brothers that he did whatever he could to interfere with our lives. He never saw that he'd be better off improving himself instead of trying to make Trevor and Kade look worse." Sawyer braced his hands on the other side of the island now. "And then he got his chance to create some real havoc. Did you know he's Harmony's father? That he seduced Cheri a week before her wedding to Kade and got her pregnant?"

"I..." Anna tore her gaze from Sawyer's with physical effort. Of course she knew. Dillon had crowed about that for eons. "I need to sit down." She lurched into the small sitting area and lowered herself into the one easy chair.

"You did know. I can see it on your face."

"It's not exactly a huge secret, Sawyer. It was all the talk of the town when I first moved here, before the gossipers found something else intriguing to focus on."

"He's dangerous, sweetheart. You need to know that. Now that he knows we're together, you'll be his target, too. He never much bothered with me before. I was just a kid when he was messing with my brothers, and then I left home. But I'm back now, and he fights dirty. And he still hates everything we Delgados stand for. He hates that we have a big, successful ranch. He hates that we have money. And he hates that my brothers are happily married."

Wouldn't it be a relief to dump the whole story in Sawyer's ears? But she couldn't. She'd already said too much.

Sawyer crouched in front of her chair and gathered her hands in his. "I'm worried about you. Promise me you won't see him again."

As if that were possible. Anna pulled her hands free and tucked them in her armpits. "I didn't plan to see him this time."

"How did he know where to find you?"

She stared past Sawyer's head.

"I need to know. Am I your baby's father, or is he?"

Ugh. Just the thought. "You. For sure."

"Then why... what does he get from all this?"

"Nothing. Sawyer, you need to go. I'm really tired."

And starving, but she didn't need an argument about her choice of ice cream.

His voice softened. "Tell me about the ultrasound."

"The baby is normal. Everything's fine."

"Are we having a boy or a girl?"

Anna's gaze snapped onto his. "*We* are not having anything, Sawyer. I've told you. The baby's sex doesn't matter."

"Do you know the answer to the question?"

"No!" She surged to her feet, nearly knocking Sawyer over. "I told the tech I don't want to know, so she didn't tell me."

"Don't I have any rights? Besides asking for a DNA test to ensure the baby is mine." He rose, facing her.

Anna glared from over by the window. "You don't believe me."

"I'm not sure I should. There have been rather a lot of surprises in the past hour, and I'm beginning to wonder what is real and what's manufactured."

She deserved that. Her shoulders slumped. "I'm pregnant. I'm not lying about that."

Sawyer nodded.

"And you're the father. I'm not lying about that, either."

CHAPTER 9

The ranch office looked out over the main corrals and barns, which made sense. The view kept Gloria connected to whatever her husband and sons were doing.

Right now, it meant Anna had a front row seat to all the action she could wish for. The rodeo events she'd watched while she tracked Sawyer had nothing on the realities of ranch life. No buzzer signaled the end of a round. The Delgado men were all in, working as a team, until they'd accomplished their goals.

November huddled against the dry cold. Snow blanketed the peaks around Eaglecrest, though nothing but a few swirls had attempted to attack the ranch.

No doubt she'd still be here when snow lay heavy and deep, secluding them even more than the distance from civilization already did. There was some allure to being trapped, even if meant her supply of tutti-frutti ice cream might be cut off. Anna had seen the cold room in what had been the original attached garage. Rows upon rows of canning jars filled with fruit and vegetables and soups and jams were a testament to Gloria's garden and hard work, and likely Ruthie and Elnora's long hours, as well. Bins of potatoes and other root vegetables anchored one corner, while multiple braids of onions and garlic hung from hooks in the adjoining nook. Huge bags of flour and sugar and oats had their own area with other dry goods, making the entire single-car bay look like a warehouse store. And then there was the walk-in freezer stuffed with packaged beef, chicken, and pork, raised right here at Eaglecrest. Thankfully, Anna had missed those particular workdays.

The Delgados were not going to starve if they were completely cut off for weeks on end, that was for sure. And there were solar panels and a backup generator to maintain at least partial power if the lines went down, which apparently wasn't particularly unusual.

A horse's high neigh and the bellows of calves drew Anna's attention back out the window. In the corral, Sawyer's lariat spun over his head then flashed out. Debonair braked to a halt as his rider leaped off amid billowing dust. When it cleared, Kade dropped beside his brother, both men obscured by the log rails.

Anna remembered to breathe. This wasn't glamorous in the least. It was hard, dangerous work. No wonder all the Delgado men, including Russ, were fit and trim. No wonder they smelled of dust and sweat and horses when they came in for meals.

Putting in such long hours meant Sawyer was too exhausted to push her right now, but that would end when the cattle liners left tomorrow, hauling last spring's calves to auction.

The brothers remounted their horses, and Sawyer looped his lariat as Debonair pivoted away.

A small noise startled Anna, and she spun in the office chair, caught staring out the window so long her computer screen had blacked out.

Instead of Gloria, Cheri stood watching her with a knowing smirk. "Our guys make a riveting sight, don't they?"

"Um... it's really interesting, what they're doing."

Cheri's grin widened as she came closer and leaned to look out the window. "Keeps my heart in my throat watching Kade out there in the middle of all those milling cattle. Accidents can happen."

Like Sawyer's friend Ace. The TV clips replayed in Anna's head often.

Cheri dropped into the other office chair and swiveled it to face Anna. "I'm glad you're here, taking some of the pressure off Gloria. And off me, since I don't know the first thing about keeping up the ranch website, and I find logging the sale details tedious. You'll have lots of entries to sort as the auction reports start coming in."

"Trevor and Denae will attend the auction, right?"

"Yeah. Russ and Gloria are going, too, since Sawyer is around to help Kade with the day-to-day stuff while they're gone." Cheri studied Anna. "Which leads me to the real reason I'm here."

"Oh?" Anna hated that her voice squeaked.

"You may know I have a history with Dillon Scarborough."

It had been too much to hope that Sawyer hadn't reported their meeting to his family. "So I've heard."

"He's Harmony's father. I'm certainly not proud of that. I was so messed up back then. I spent six years trying to get away from him and stay off his radar, but he was determined not to leave Harmony and me alone. He's a mean, manipulative man."

Not much Anna could argue with there, so she nodded.

"I don't know what your connection is to Dillon, but I beg you to cut him out of your life. If he's told you he loves you, know that he loves no one but himself. If he promises you stuff, he has no means to fulfill his promises."

Except he did.

"My brother-in-law is worth twenty of Dillon. I can't understand why you won't accept Sawyer. He loves you, you know."

Tears sprang to Anna's eyes. Love. What did that even mean?

"The Delgado men love deep, Anna. They love forever. Kade never throws my past into my face, even though I cheated him out of six years together. Even though I returned with Dillon's child, Kade loved me like God loves us. We've all looked God in the face, one way or another, and rejected His love. Gone on and done our own thing. But when we turn back to Him, we find Him waiting with arms outstretched to welcome us into the fold."

"I went to church in Bozeman. Denae and Lauren invited me a few times here, but I wasn't ready." Man, she'd been stupid. Think of all the life-altering mistakes she could have avoided. "God's love is… pretty cool."

Cheri studied her. "Have you asked for His forgiveness for going your own way and rejecting Him? Is He King of your life now?"

"He's forgiven me. I know that, but it doesn't change anything." Anna rubbed her palms over her belly. "I'm still pregnant." Still holding secrets like a cloak around her, because what were the alternatives? She knew what she was really like.

"You're wrong. God's love changes everything. I had a really hard time with that, too, so I get it. Plus, Dillon has a way of messing with a girl's head. But, if you're following the Lord, you must see that Dillon has no place in your future. Sawyer—"

An uproar from the corral offered a welcome diversion. Anna swung her chair back to the window as Cheri leaned over the desk beside her, peering out. A moment later the dust cleared. Sawyer sprang back into his saddle, and Debonair surged forward.

Anna dared a breath. She couldn't love Sawyer. She couldn't throw herself on his mercy. He'd never forgive her. Even God was giving her a side-eye.

And it would be too hard watching the man she loved put himself in danger every single day.

That was the whole thing, really. She'd never expected to fall in love with Sawyer Delgado, but she was halfway there.

SAWYER STOOD BESIDE HIS BROTHER, waving as the two cattle liners pulled away from the corral's loading chutes and began their trek down River Road. Trevor had shot out the drive ahead of them, in a hurry to get home to Denae for their trip to the auction in Missoula. No doubt the guy wanted a shower first.

That's where Dad was. He and Mom would be gone within the half hour and were not expected back until late tomorrow, or maybe even the next day if they hadn't had a chance to load up on farm supplies yet. A lot depended on which point in the auction Eaglecrest calves landed.

Kade clapped him on the shoulder. "Need me to stick around?"

"For what?"

"Chaperone, of course. Or to keep a shotgun loaded in case Scarborough decides to show up."

"I don't need a chaperone. It's not like Anna is even speaking to me. Besides, Ruthie and Elnora are here, and Max is sticking around the barns, too." Sawyer scowled. "And if that lowlife shows his ugly face, he won't get far."

"You can't be too careful."

"I know it." He'd been too complacent until two days ago. Given time, Anna would see he was steady and devoted. Scarborough had added urgency. Doubt.

"Want me and Cheri and the kids to take our meals here?"

"Pretty sure your wife would like to see you around a bit more after the last couple of busy weeks."

Kade smirked. "Possibly."

"Don't worry about me. Just... pray for Anna." The

words still sounded like a foreign phrase rolling from his tongue.

"You've got it. Did I tell you Cheri talked to her about Dillon yesterday?"

Sawyer pivoted and narrowed his gaze at his brother. "Why is she interfering?"

"She's not." Kade met his gaze solid. "You're not the only one with a stake in this game. You're my little brother. The baby she's carrying is my nephew or niece... unless it's Harmony's half-sibling."

"She swears the baby is mine." But the thought she might also have been with Dillon punched Sawyer like a fist in a bar-fight. Not that he'd believed for a minute he was the only guy she'd ever slept with, just as Anna knew she hadn't been his first. But that the other guy was Scarborough? The only devastation that could compare was seeing Ace trampled beneath the bronc's sharp hooves.

"So, yeah, we're praying. Believe me. But we're also not going to stand by and let you two go through this alone if there's anything we can do." Kade's gaze was hard and steady. "This affects all of us. It's an assault on not just you, but the Delgado family."

"Do you think...?" But, no. That was stupid. Farfetched. Scarborough was nothing beyond an opportunist. The guy had so few brain cells they barely bumped into each other in his cavernous skull.

"Think what?"

Sawyer shook his head. "Never mind. Max and I can handle the chores tonight." He nodded toward the corral, where the big John Deere had already been fired up. "In fact, he's totally on it already."

"Give me a call if you need anything. And I do mean *anything*."

"Yeah. Thanks. But we're good."

"Okay." Kade gave him a sharp nod then strode over and jumped on his four-wheeler. Within seconds, the whining sound of the engine had disappeared down the shortcut to the house Kade had built Cheri overlooking the river.

Mom came out of the house towing her luggage.

"I'll get that," called Sawyer as he jogged over. He loaded it into the backseat of his parents' truck. "Anything else?"

"I could have managed fine." Mom laughed and angled her face toward the high valleys beyond the ranch. "We're heading out in just a few minutes, but I've got to say, I'm a bit concerned about the weather. The forecast is clear, but the view up there doesn't look clear to me."

Sawyer followed her gaze. A few dark clouds hung low in the distance. "It'll probably blow over."

"Looks like snow to me."

He shrugged. "Could be. We're about due. I'm just glad we got the calves to market before it hit."

"We cut it a bit close this year. But calf prices have held steady for the past few weeks, so we should do okay at auction even though we're a little late." Mom turned back to Sawyer. "You sure you're okay here without us?"

"What am I, twelve? Everything's fine. You've left me the full contingent of staff, and Kade's just down the road.

And you'll be gone for a day or two at most. I'm not sure what you think I could screw up in that short of time."

"Anna..." Mom pursed her lips. "Tread carefully, son."

And this was why he'd stayed away as much as he could for ten years. This whole baby-of-the-family thing where he was an irresponsible schmuck. "I've got it, Mom."

"That's what I'm worried about."

His eyebrows shot up. "I beg your pardon?"

"It's God who needs to have it, Sawyer. Not you."

"That's what I meant." Wasn't it?

Dad came down the stone steps by the front door. "I was going to get that suitcase, Gloria."

Mom shrugged. "If it makes you feel any better, Sawyer put it in the truck."

"Much better." Dad slid his arm around Mom's waist and kissed her hair. "Thanks, Sawyer. You okay with—"

"The road's calling you. Get out of here already." Sawyer pointed down the drive. "Give me a call and let me know how the auction went."

"You've got it." Dad opened the truck's passenger door and handed Mom up into the seat. "Take care." He nodded to Sawyer as he rounded the vehicle.

Why did nobody think he could manage the ranch for a couple of days? Sawyer stepped aside and waved as his parents' truck rolled out of the yard.

The rumble of the tractor hauling a round bale of hay was barely discernible amid the clamor of cows who missed their calves. He was going to need earplugs to sleep tonight.

He should warn Anna.

CHAPTER 10

Anna woke to the same sound she'd fallen asleep to: the baying of cows deprived of their young. But there was something different about it now. The sound had been somehow muted. Deadened.

She opened her eyes to a faint rectangle of light from her window, but a squint at her clock revealed only darkness. The power was out, which would explain the cold nip at her nose.

No. She'd fall back asleep. It couldn't be full morning yet, or the sky would be brighter. When she awoke next time, the power would be back. Right? She snuggled down under the soft duvet, but her mind drove the miles of River Road as it wound and climbed into the mountains, lined by an equal number of miles of power lines.

There was a reason for the solar panels and generators. Were they enough to run the office computers, or might she get the day off to enjoy her cozy apartment away from

Sawyer? Scratch that. It wasn't cozy and likely wouldn't be until hours after the power returned.

She wouldn't be able to cook. Her ice cream would melt, though it seemed likely it was cold enough to prevent that.

Anna groaned and pushed back the duvet. What time *was* it? She popped the button on her watch to illuminate the dial. Seven forty? Really? She wedged her feet into slippers, wrapped her robe tight, then made her way over to the living room window overlooking the ranch yard.

It was pristine... and covered with what looked like two feet of snow. Beautiful, but not a welcome sight. Out of her line of sight, she heard the tractor growling over near the corrals.

Ranch work never stopped. There were no true days off around here, except for maybe in the office.

She couldn't shower, but she'd be warmer in leggings and a long sweater than her jammies and robe. After changing, she brushed her hair and pulled it into a ponytail. The power hadn't flickered. Not that she'd expected it to.

Someone pounded on the door at the bottom of the stairs, then boots stomped in the entryway. "Anna? You okay?" Sawyer. Of course, he'd check on her.

She walked to the top of the steps, shivering. "It's cold."

"Come on over to the house. Max fired up the generator to power the necessities, and the kitchen stove's propane, so Ruthie's fixing breakfast. We'll build a fire in the great room."

Anna stared down at him. She'd never seen him with something on his head other than his Stetson, but today he wore a knit cap with a dusting of snow clinging to it. He'd ditched his denim jacket for a puffy parka.

Sawyer's invitation sounded idyllic if she really wanted a cozy day with him. The problem was, she did. At least, if she could forget all the reasons she couldn't relax and enjoy it.

"It's only going to get colder in here, sweetheart. We don't have the resources to keep the whole ranch powered up."

She wasn't going to freeze to death because of principle. That was just stupid. "Will my fridge stuff be okay?"

Sawyer's eyebrows shot up. "Worried about your ice cream?"

Honesty was the best policy, at least where possible. "Well, maybe..."

"It will be fine. We'll check occasionally to make sure. We'll only be across at the house. And don't worry about the waterlines. There's a dedicated solar battery heating the pipes. It stores up enough juice for a few days, anyway."

"What should I bring?"

"You're dressed for it. That's good. So just whatever you need for the day. If you need to spend the night at the house, we can come back and grab more supplies."

Oh, that better not happen. He'd mentioned warming only the central part of the sprawling ranch house. That wouldn't include the upstairs bedrooms, though the room she'd stayed in a couple of weeks ago had its own fireplace. So, maybe...?

No use thinking of that right now. She turned to gather her phone and laptop. Then she descended the steps to where Sawyer held her jacket out for her. She slipped her arms into the sleeves, shivering as his hands settled the collar across her shoulders.

The snow across the parking lot came nearly to her knees. She slipped once, and Sawyer's strong hand caught her elbow. A minute later, he opened the house door and ushered her into the relative warmth of his parents' large home.

"Ready for some breakfast, Miss Anna?" Ruthie leaned around the corner from the kitchen.

"Thanks so much. Yes, I'm hungry." As always, these days. Maybe today wouldn't be so bad if Ruthie and Elnora were nearby.

"Pull up a chair. I'll be just a minute."

They shed their outerwear and entered the breakfast room where Sawyer seated her. Then he poured two cups of coffee while Ruthie dumped sausages into her skillet.

"Are power outages common here?" Anna rubbed her arms. The air might be warmer than the garage apartment, but it wasn't as pleasant as usual.

"Fairly." Sawyer splashed some cream into one of the mugs and brought them both to the table. He sat around the corner from her. "Eaglecrest often has to fend for itself for a few days once or twice most winters."

A few days? The shock must have shown on her face, because Sawyer chuckled.

"Yeah, we're in for it this time, I think. This storm wasn't even in yesterday's forecast. Maybe it's rain down in the valley. That often happens this time of year."

"It puts me to mind of the year Miss Cheri came

home." Ruthie's spatula scraped the cast iron frying pan, and the aroma of spicy pork sausage filled the air. "The lines were down for the better part of a week that Thanksgiving."

"Dad baked the pumpkin pies in the grill." Sawyer chuckled. "And no one got to watch the football game."

Ruthie scooped a handful of chopped vegetables into the skillet, and Anna took a sip of her coffee. Sawyer had managed the exact right amount of cream. "Thanks."

His eyebrows peaked. "For...?"

Fixing her coffee right? Taking care of her in a snowstorm? Getting her pregnant? She shrugged and turned to Ruthie. "What are your plans for today?"

The middle-aged cook snagged a carton of eggs from the fridge. "Not much. I was going to start on some of the holiday baking, but there's no point in that with the power out. I'll likely ask Sawyer here to haul in an armload or two of logs to keep the fire going in the little sitting room. Elnora and I are figuring to crochet up a stack of baby blankets for the hospital auxiliary gift shop this winter, so we may as well get started."

"Sounds lovely." Maybe she could buy one to send with the baby.

"Do you crochet? You could join us."

"I don't. Sorry." Though that would keep her out of Sawyer's way. A quick glance at him showed he'd read her mind.

"Here now." Ruthie scooped breakfast onto two plates and brought them to the table. "Don't you worry about lunch. I'll be back out to fix something." She looked between them. "If you need anything, you know where to find us."

"I'll fill up your wood box shortly, Ruthie."

The breakfast looked and smelled amazing. Anna reached for her fork, but Sawyer's hand captured hers. "Lord, I thank you for today..."

Was he just thankful to be stranded with her? At least they were in no danger of freezing to death or worse, starving. She pulled her hand free the instant he uttered his amen.

"READY FOR AN ADVENTURE?" Sawyer dropped a load of logs on the great room hearth and glanced at Anna.

She was snuggled under one of Elnora's afghans in the armchair nearest the fireplace, but her eyes narrowed on his. "What do you have in mind?"

Kissing.

Wrong answer, which was why he'd needed to come up with an actual plan besides simply hanging out together. "Thought I'd hitch Nip and Tuck to the sleigh, and we could drive over to Kade and Cheri's."

"A sleigh ride? Behind horses?"

Bingo. He hadn't missed the spark of interest. "The very same. I gave my brother a call and he——"

"I thought the lines were down."

He held up his cell phone. "Satellite service."

"Oh." She studied him, worrying her bottom lip with her teeth. "It sounds cold."

Sawyer forced his gaze away from her lips. They really, really needed an activity or he couldn't guarantee his distance. *I can do all things through God who gives me strength.* And he'd need that strength. Wouldn't it be better not to put himself in temptation's way? "Cold for a little while, but it will be worth it. Cheri's put on a big pot of chili already, simmering on their wood cookstove, so it's no extra work for her. I just need to be back before dark so I can give Max a hand with evening chores. What do you say?"

"Sure, why not?" She threw back the afghan and unfolded her legs.

"If you don't have snow pants, you can wear a pair of my mom's. They should be in the closet in the back hall-way." He knelt to shove a split log into the fireplace. Make that two.

Anna rose from the armchair and paused behind him. His body tensed, hyper aware, but he didn't look up at her.

"I don't know why you're so nice to me. After the other day."

Sawyer rose slowly and turned.

She looked so vulnerable, so sad, all he wanted to do was hold her close and kiss her fears away, whatever they were. "Anna, I..." How could he make her understand? "We got off to a bad start in June." He motioned toward her belly. "I'm sorry. I don't know how to convince you I mean it. I should be more sorry about the baby. I know that, but honestly? I'm incredibly glad that it brought you back into my life. I want to prove to you that you can trust me, that I won't do anything to hurt you or our child. Not on purpose, anyway."

Anna tightened her arms around her middle. "Thank you."

Hope surged. "Will you marry me? Let me provide for you and our baby?"

She shook her head, just barely. "It's not that easy, Sawyer."

"But why not?" He cupped her shoulders. "It's the only way through this that makes any sense to me. I don't want to give you up again. I don't want our baby to be placed with someone else. We can do this, sweetheart. Together."

Anna took half a step back, just far enough to pull from his light grasp. "I can't. I'd be a terrible mother."

"No, you wouldn't be. I know it."

"Going to your brother's house is a good idea." She pivoted toward the doorway. "We should do that now."

She was shutting him down. Again. Two of the ten weeks he'd bargained for were already gone and a third was well on its way. Panic clawed up his throat. He could lose her forever. Could lose his child forever. *God, help me!*

How could God stand by and let this happen? It was the same God who didn't waken Ace from the coma in which he slept. The same God who'd let Kade's first wife, Daniela, die after giving birth to Jericho. The same God who let Cheri run from Dillon in panic for six entire years.

Sawyer had told Anna she could trust him.

Proverbs 3:5-6 told him he could count on God. *Trust in the Lord with all your heart, and do not lean on your own understanding. In all your ways acknowledge him, and he will make straight your paths.*

Today, right now, it was mighty hard to hang onto that.

Where was the proof that Anna would come to love him? Where was the proof that Dillon wouldn't win? Where was the proof that God had Sawyer's back?

He hadn't grown up in a Christian home for nothing — church every week, Sunday school then youth group as he got older. Hebrews 6 sprang to mind. *Faith is the assurance of things hoped for, the conviction of things not seen... without faith it is impossible to please him, for whoever would draw near to God must believe that he exists and that he rewards those who seek him.*

The hall closet doors rattled, pulling Sawyer back to the moment.

Faith. Trust. Was he really up for this, no matter what?

CHAPTER 11

"M iss Anna! Duck!" Harmony yelled as she dove behind the barricade of snow she'd helped Anna and Cheri pack together.

But Anna was too far from the meager shelter. A snowball smacked against her back and shattered. She bent to scoop a handful of snow and fling it over her shoulder, but small arms caught at her hips, and down she went, Jericho on her legs.

"I got her, Uncle Sawyer!" Jericho crowed.

Anna rolled over and flicked snow at the little guy's face. "Got you back!"

He giggled and twisted away from her just as strong arms captured her from behind and hoisted her upward.

"I didn't mean to make you fall. You okay?"

She shivered at Sawyer's warm breath right by her ear. "I'm fine." How could she feel his strength against her body through both of their padded bib overalls and parkas? But she did.

"Maybe you should rest for a few minutes."

Like forever. Right here in his steady hold.

A few feet away, Jericho tackled his sister, and the two of them wrestled in the snow. Their little brother toddled over, tripped, and tumbled on top of them, squealing.

Once she'd dreamed of a family like this of her own, but then she'd realized Mom had been right. Winter women made poor choices. They were lousy mothers. Not such great humans, all told.

"No, I'm fine." She pulled out of his arms but made the mistake of looking at him.

Sawyer's deep dark eyes seemed softer, somehow, as they searched her face. More vulnerable. "I don't want anything to happen to you. To the baby."

She'd been guilty of wishing something would, especially in the early days when the puking had been all too real and the realization of what she'd done and still must do had slammed her upside the head.

Anna took a deep breath. She could never forget for long, but the few minutes had been wonderful while they lasted. "Maybe I will go sit down on the steps."

Sawyer's hand at her elbow steadied her as she plowed through the uneven snow, the once-smooth surface broken from so much running and tussling.

She'd no sooner taken a seat when Cheri dropped beside her. "Did Jer get you too hard?"

"No. The snow is soft. I'm fine. It's just that I spend too much time sitting at a desk and not enough getting exercise. And it's hard to run in two feet of snow."

Cheri chuckled. "I get more exercise than I ever

dreamed of. Those three keep me on my feet and thinking fast."

Jericho attacked Sawyer, who pivoted and grabbed his nephew. He flung the boy over his shoulder and tromped over into unmarred snow then dropped him on his back. Jericho flailed, shrieking and giggling.

"He'll be a good dad. Our kids adore him."

Even though Sawyer's sister-in-law was absolutely correct, there was no point in agreeing verbally. That would only lead to the obvious questions. Ones Anna couldn't answer, since it was too bad his baby had a poor excuse for a mother.

Cheri's elbow nudged Anna's arm. "Would it be so terrible to say yes?" she asked quietly.

Jericho grabbed Sawyer's knit cap and threw it into the snow. The kid hadn't stopped laughing in probably ten minutes.

It would be wonderful to say yes in so many ways.

"I can't."

"You know, I really resented Harmony when she was a baby." Cheri clasped her fuzzy red mittens together. "All I ever saw when I looked at her was Dillon's face. All I saw was how badly I'd messed up. It wasn't her fault. She'd done nothing to deserve the mess she was born into."

"Were you... a bad mom?"

Cheri sighed. "In some ways, yeah. I mean, babies need love. I tried so hard not to love Harmony."

"My mom didn't love me." Now why had she gone and mentioned that? These weren't words she went around saying to just anyone. And Sawyer's sister-in-law should be about the second last person she said them to. Someone who'd been wronged by Dillon.

"I don't remember mine." Cheri stared blankly out across the yard.

Anna would hazard a guess she wasn't seeing her kids dog-piling on the men. "Did she die?" Or worse?

"She and my dad both, in a traffic accident. I was quite young. My grandparents raised me."

"I'm sorry."

"It had its moments, for sure. And my grandparents were no spring chickens when I showed up. They did their best, but it wasn't the same as parents who wanted me."

Anna's grandmother had been an alcoholic. Mom had followed in her mother's footsteps. Anna had avoided that particular trap, at least so far.

Cheri cast her a sideways look. "That's one thing I appreciate so much about my in-laws. Gloria and Russ lead by example. They love the Lord and their sons. They're the family I never had growing up."

An ache seized Anna's heart. "I thought they'd kick me out when Sawyer brought me home." She wished they had, because walking away at the end of the year was going to be like amputating a limb. Like purposefully walking from light to darkness. From blissful sunshine to a blinding blizzard.

"They'd never do that. They're so full of grace, and they love Sawyer too much."

"I know that now." But it didn't change anything in the end. It didn't change who Anna was.

"Kade and I were talking the other night..."

Cheri's words trailed off. Did Anna want to know the end of the thought? Probably not. It sounded too cozy. She gathered herself to stand, but Cheri's hand rested on Anna's sleeve.

"Hear me out?"

Anna sank back. What was going on?

"We were wondering... if you absolutely for certain are putting the baby up for adoption... if there's any chance you'd consider us."

What? What was she hearing? No way. This was crazy. Ludicrous. Insane, even. "No."

Cheri met her gaze, eyes full of compassion.

Anna was certain hers were wide with shock.

"I know this came out of nowhere to you, but think about it. Pray about it. We could do an open adoption, so you could be part of the baby's life—"

"No." She surged to her feet and stood there, swaying. "Just, no."

Before she could form another thought, another sentence, Sawyer was beside her, arm supporting her. "What's going on?"

Cheri rose. "I just—"

"She wants to take the baby." Anna closed her eyes. Why wouldn't the world stop spinning?

"Take?" Sawyer sounded confused.

"Kade and I are willing to adopt—"

Sawyer growled. "I told him to drop that stupid idea."

"But—"

Anna whirled to face him. "You knew about this?"

Sawyer held her up. "I thought I'd put a stop to it." He glared at his sister-in-law. "I told Kade no."

Cheri twisted her mittened hands together. "We just thought—"

Sawyer's hand sliced through the air. "*Praying* is good. Great, even. But stop with the thinking. It's not your problem to solve."

Kade stepped up beside Cheri and rested his arm across her shoulders.

Sawyer jabbed his gloved fist at his brother's chest. "I told you to stay out of it."

Kade stumbled back a step. "You did. Sorry. But I stand with my wife. We are willing to adopt your baby." He looked hard at Sawyer then focused on Anna, his gaze softening slightly. "Family sticks together. Helps each other."

Some did. Hers didn't. Not the one in her past, certainly, and there wasn't one in her future.

SAWYER FLICKED the reins over Nip's and Tuck's backs. "Walk on."

The bells on their harnesses jingled as the Percheron pair tossed their heads and stepped out.

He should rip those stupid bells off. They inferred 'making spirits bright,' to say nothing of 'laughing all the way.' They did not match the dark fury spinning in his head that Kade had gone against his clearly expressed wishes.

Anna sat on the other end of the sleigh's seat, as far away from him as she could get in the limited space. Her face might as well have been set in stone with its clenched jaw and unblinking gaze as she stared straight ahead. Except... was that a tear snaking down her cheek?

His rage subsided as quickly as the storm after Jesus calmed it. In full force one instant, completely gone the next. "Look. I'm sorry."

"I can't believe they'd think that was a good solution!" She turned to him as her arms circled her belly, anger burning in her hazel eyes.

"I know." The thought of watching his brother raise Sawyer's child nearly cleaved him in two. A little boy with dark hair like Donovan calling Kade *Daddy* and Cheri *Mommy*. But was it worse than knowing his son didn't know him at all? Called strangers his parents?

No. A thousand times no. That little life belonged to him. How could he give it up to anyone else besides Anna? It was unfathomable.

"Why does God hate me so much?"

Her whimper was so faint Sawyer wasn't sure he'd even heard it at first, but a glance across the sleigh seat revealed Anna curled forward, her hair veiling her face, her knit cap skewed sideways. But the real giveaway was her shaking shoulders.

"Sweetheart, God doesn't hate you." How could he get through to her? "You're His precious child. He loves you. He'd do anything for you." Just like Sawyer would do anything to protect that life growing in Anna's womb.

"It's so hard."

His heart broke all over again. What could he say? For a moment he stared between Tuck's ears as he and Nip followed the faintly visible trail from this morning. More snow had fallen, the limbs of the firs and spruces sagging under the white weight.

"God is our Father, Anna. I'm beginning to understand that love."

"Don't..."

"I want to marry you, sweetheart. We can raise our baby together. It's the best way."

"We can't. It's not."

Oh, God, help me here. How can this not be Your will?

Could something be God's will and yet be thwarted by a human's will? Before, he might have laughed at the thought. God was sovereign, after all. Of course, His will would prevail. But then, what of all the turmoil in the world?

No. He'd given humans free will, and they'd made the most of it. He, Sawyer Delgado, had made the most of it. And an innocent spark of life was one result.

"You know my family." All the good, bad, and the ugly. "Tell me about yours." Maybe that would help him understand.

Anna rocked in her seat, shoulders still trembling.

"Sweetheart, what's *your* daddy like?"

She turned to look at him, her eyes bleak, her chin quivering. "I don't know."

Sawyer snapped his mouth shut and held her gaze. "What happened?"

"He wasn't the staying kind, I guess." Her voice broke.

"Oh, sweetheart." Sawyer slid over the wooden bench and slipped his arm around her. Thankfully the Percherons knew their way home.

Anna leaned against him as he rubbed his gloved hand up and down her arm.

Please, Lord. "Don't judge all men by your father. We're not all like him. I'm the staying kind. I promise."

She straightened, pulling away from him, except she'd fall off the sleigh if she went any further. "I'm not the kind of woman a man would stay for."

Sawyer looked at her, his mouth dropping open. "How can you say that? You're everything a man could want."

"I'm not. I'm too much like my mother."

"Oh, Anna. If you're like her, she must be wonderful. A paragon."

A bitter laugh escaped. "She's an alcoholic who sleeps around and can't keep a job, Sawyer."

"But you're not like that at all." Sure, they'd had some drinks together back in June, but that didn't make her an addict. And sleeping with him didn't mean she'd welcome just any guy, anytime. Did it? Best not to dwell on that. "You had that job at the Branding Iron for, what, three years?"

"I'm like her inside."

This demanded all his attention. "Hup, hup, whoa."

The Percherons' ears flickered at the command and, within a few steps, they came to a complete halt.

Sawyer turned to Anna. "Look at me, sweetheart."

She glanced at him but didn't seem able to hold the connection.

"You told me you'd come to the Lord in Bozeman. That you'd prayed for salvation. What did Jesus do for you?"

"He-He saved me. Forgave me."

"From what?"

Anna's cheeks pinked, but it might have been the cold. "For being pregnant. For being a selfish girl who—" She bit off her words.

"We're all selfish, sweetheart. We all think of ourselves first. I was only thinking of myself in June." He pulled off his glove and touched her face. Felt the chill where her tears had frozen. "I wasn't thinking of you. I'm sorry."

"I just..." She shook her head. "It's not that easy."

"You keep saying that, but it *is* that simple. Jesus didn't pick and choose which of our sins to die for. He took them all. Redeemed them all." Sawyer's own heart lifted a little at the thought. He'd certainly tested that doctrine of the faith and experienced it in his own life. He'd messed up in so many ways. Knew the truth but went willfully on his way.

He was forgiven. But consequences remained. This time around, he couldn't help but be a little glad for that. At least, if Anna would agree to his solution. It was the only one.

Sawyer smoothed his thumb over her cheekbone. "Anna, sweetheart. Marry me. Please."

"I can't," she whispered. Fresh tears glistened on her eyelashes. "Can we go home now?"

At least she'd called Eaglecrest home. Sawyer swallowed the lump in his throat and gathered the reins. "Walk on."

CHAPTER 12

Anna stuck close to Ruthie or Elnora all the next day. The snow stopped falling around noon. Sawyer plowed out the yard then started down River Road, which at least kept him out of her hair for a few hours. By late afternoon, the state's highway equipment had met the ranch tractor, the road was cleared, and Russ and Gloria had made it home. The power popped back on as Ruthie prepared supper.

Life was back to normal, only with two feet of snow, and tomorrow she'd be back in the office logging the auction stats into the database.

If only her gut would quit quivering. She'd been so on edge with Cheri and Kade's offer then the confrontation with Sawyer. The tension couldn't be good for her. Couldn't be good for the baby.

Ruthie had put her to work peeling carrots, but Anna leaned against the counter for a minute. Her belly pushed back. She stared down at the bulge that no amount of pretending could dismiss anymore. There it was again. She touched it. Just a little flutter. Only nervousness? Or something else...

"You okay, hon?" Gloria paused nearby with her hand on the faucet.

Anna met her gaze. "I'm not sure."

"What is it?"

"Th-the baby."

Instantly, she had Sawyer's mom's full attention. "Pain? Or what?"

"No." Anna looked down at her hand on the little bulge. There it was again, like a tumble in her tummy. She looked up in wonder.

Gloria offered a soft smile. "The baby moving around?"

"Is that—?" It had to be.

"Like a butterfly dance at first."

Anna nodded, staring past Gloria out the breakfast room window. "I can't believe..."

"Can't believe what, hon?"

She couldn't say it out loud. Maybe if she'd read about pregnancy, studied up what was coming, she wouldn't have been so surprised, but she'd been working on the blind assumption that what she didn't know couldn't affect her. The baby wasn't real.

Suddenly, it was.

There was more going on than a lack of periods and a positive pee test. More than hormones that yanked her emotions every which way. More than a blob of tissue. Oh, she'd known all that. Only, now, she *knew*.

The full weight of the knowledge crashed into her, and she swayed.

"Have a seat, hon. I'll finish up the carrots."

"No, I can..."

"I know you can, but I don't mind. Take a minute to savor what's going on."

Anna looked at Gloria with new insight. This woman had carried three sons. She'd felt Sawyer somersault in her womb. Had he been active? Had Gloria known he'd be a boy, solid and strong?

Had she bonded with him even before his birth?

Because, try as Anna might to avoid them, links were forming. It was as though the baby's arms and legs were rapidly growing vines winding around her heart. Clinging to her. Tying her and Sawyer together with unbreakable bonds. "No."

But Gloria took her arm and guided her around the corner into the great room. "I'll make you a cup of tea." She nudged her into an armchair then whisked away.

Anna stared into the crackling fire, her emotions a matching conflagration, as though that were anything new. This changed everything. Everything except who she was. Who her mother was. What her heritage was.

She bent to cover her face with both hands. Tears seeped between her fingers as her shoulders shook. *Oh, God...*

A door shut in the distance. Boots stomped on the stone floor in the back entry followed by thuds as the boots came off. Low voices came from the kitchen. A moment later, a cup clinked on the little table beside her.

Sawyer's arm slid across her shoulders as he knelt at her side, his hair tousled where his Stetson had been. He rubbed her upper arm, up and down, up and down, a soothing motion. "What's wrong, sweetheart?"

Anna's fire had fizzled. She was so tired of pushing him away, of telling him not to call her that. She longed for it to be as real as the baby they had made. Just for this moment she'd lean against him. She curled her face into the crook of his neck.

In an instant she was wrapped in his arms, pressed against his chest. His hands were in her hair, down her back, stroking, comforting. "Oh, Anna."

He felt so good. So solid. So caring.

"Talk to me, sweetheart," he murmured against her temple.

"I felt the baby move," she whispered.

If it were possible, he clutched her tighter then pressed a kiss to her hair. "Can I feel?"

"I... I don't know." She caught her breath. "It was only a little flutter."

Sawyer pulled back enough to look in her eyes. His were full of wonder and... could that shimmer be a tear or two? No. A strong man like him wouldn't cry. He rested his hand on the little bump.

The touch was so intimate, so tender, that Anna couldn't breathe. Neither could she look away as the baby shifted again. "Feel that?"

He shook his head. "No," he whispered. "Was there something?"

Anna tugged his hand over an inch or two, their fingers meeting and linking.

"I don't feel anything," he said in a low voice, his head tilting toward hers. And then, gaze still intense, his mouth brushed hers.

Her free hand found its way around his neck, fingering the short hairs at his nape as she caught at his lips with hers. Her eyes drifted closed.

With a groan he captured her mouth, and she gave herself in to his kiss.

If only. If only.

HE HADN'T KNOWN he could feel this deeply. Macho cowboys didn't do emotions. Didn't do touchy-feely. But he couldn't get enough of this woman. It wasn't just the physical rush as she responded to his kisses. It was more. Deeper.

He was in love.

Sawyer rocked back on his heels, loosening his hold but not letting go. He drank in the sight of her, blond hair slightly tousled where he'd run his fingers through it, lips full and pink where he'd crushed them. Her hazel eyes, now wide with... something. "Anna?"

"I wish..." Her gaze dropped, maybe to their hands still entwined over her belly. "I wish things were different."

Him, too, but he wasn't one for staring into the past. Nothing back there mattered in the saddle of a wild bronc, not when focus on each microsecond was vital. He'd lived his entire life with that intensity since he'd been a rough-and-tumble kid tagging behind his big brothers. Aside from a few unrelenting goals — like that ever-elusive championship trophy — he hadn't looked far into the future, either.

Of course, his absorption with the present at the expense of past and future was also how he'd gotten into this mess. A guy who didn't look back didn't learn from his mistakes. A guy who didn't look forward didn't think of consequences.

"Different is an option." Sawyer slid his palm down her cheek. "Marry me, sweetheart."

Her back stiffened as she pulled her hand from his, locking both of hers together. She stared downward. "But it's not."

"I don't understand. Am I so terrible?" What a way to sell himself to her. Where was his confidence? She'd all but pummeled it out of him with her refusal to consider marriage. More like her stalwart resistance was a wall that refused to break no matter what he threw at it.

"No." Anna inhaled a ragged breath. "It's not you. It's me."

"That's a tired old line." He kept his voice as light as he could with her visibly pulling away from him once again.

"That doesn't make it less true. You don't even know me. Not really."

He'd known her in the biblical sense of the word, but this might not be the time to bring that up. "I'd like to. Every time I ask about your family, your childhood, you change the subject."

Sawyer had only realized it yesterday when she'd actually let something slip about her mother. Selfish guy that he was, living in the present, he hadn't given a lot of thought to Anna's history. Didn't it stand to reason her background had made her who she was today? Well, except for pregnant. That was all on him.

She surged to her feet, nearly toppling him over from where he'd squatted by her chair. "Do you think the apartment is heating up now that the power's back? I should go see."

"I'll go have a look." He rose beside her and reached for her hands. "I'll check the waterlines while I'm out there."

"Stop, Sawyer." Anna tucked her hands behind herself and took a step back. "Stop trying to fix things."

"Never." He held her gaze until she tore it away. "It's who I am. Besides, I'm the one who got you pregnant. It's up to me to find a solution, and what could be better than marriage and making a family together?"

A tear glinted on her cheek, but she didn't swipe at it.

That meant he had to. He was a fixer, right? So he reached out and brushed it away. "Don't cry, sweetheart. Just say yes. It will all be okay."

Anna's jaw tensed.

He might not have noticed if he hadn't been touching her cheek. Now his hand dropped away. What on earth was holding her back? This was getting ridiculous. She'd been at Eaglecrest for four weeks, and time was slipping through his fingers. Anna might relent for an occasional kiss — just often enough to keep his hopes up — but the tenderness he'd been striving to show her wasn't enough. There was only so much rejection a man could take.

"Anna, seriously. What's going on here?" This time his exasperation leaked out. "How can I fight this if I'm in the dark?"

"It's not your fight." She put a bit of distance between them.

Nope. That was not all right. He closed the gap. "Anna, talk to me."

"Talking doesn't solve problems."

What? Sawyer felt his eyebrows shoot up. "That's ridiculous. It's called negotiation. It's called putting your cards on the table. I may be better at kissing than talking, but that doesn't mean I don't know it's important. How in blazes can a guy deal with veiled hints and mystery words like you're throwing at me? Just give it to me straight, whatever it is." He stared hard at her. "And let me fix it."

She whirled away from him and dashed into the entry.

He watched helplessly as she stuffed her feet into her boots, grabbed her parka, and flew out the door. It smacked shut behind her.

Way to go, Delgado. Sawyer rubbed his temples with both hands and tried to get in a few solid breaths. Where was the precision focus he'd honed in rodeo? The mustang was a coiled spring between his thighs in the chute. Sawyer was in the saddle, braided rope gathered in his left hand, his right high. He marked the horse out, offered a terse nod, and the gate opened. The bronc shot into the arena, determined to unseat him with all the twists and bucks and kicks it could muster. Sawyer clung to his seat while spurring the horse to greater feats.

Eight seconds. He only had to stay aboard for eight seconds, and do it with flair.

That was rodeo. *This* was life, and it didn't play out in eight-second blips.

Ace Desjardins hadn't lasted three on his final ride, but the memory replayed in Sawyer's mind in slo-mo. Ace had drawn Cramer, the highest ranked gelding in the pens that day. He'd swaggered around the ready area, smack-talking his intent to win the event.

Adam Cavanagh had gone first, racking up a solid 82 points. A few other riders rode lower scores before Desjardins headed for the shoot. Cavanagh punched Ace's shoulder. "Beat that."

"Easy as stealing candy from a baby."

It had not been. Desjardins had made a fatal error in judgment the instant Cramer broke through the gate. Yeah, he'd marked out, but the bronc had somehow caught him off guard even so.

Sawyer would never forget the crack of Desjardins' skull on the rump of the horse. Never forget the sight of his friend's body sliding to the dirt. The pick-up man had arrived a fraction of a second too late to divert Cramer before his hooves descended on the inert rider.

Cold sweat saturated Sawyer's shirt even now at the memory. He tried to force the images away, but they clung. He remembered his own ride in the hushed arena a few minutes later. Just like every cowboy who'd ridden after

Ace, he'd been rattled. He'd lasted five seconds before hitting the dirt. Disqualified.

He was still rattled.

Adam Cavanagh took the prize, but there'd been no glory in it.

"Son? Where did Anna go?"

Sawyer scrubbed his temples one more time and turned slowly to face his mother. "Out to the apartment to see if the heat kicked in." His voice sounded dull even to himself.

"Are you okay?"

"Define okay." A harsh laugh erupted. "Nothing's okay."

"There was kissing..." Mom's voice was suggestive.

"It means nothing to her." But it did. He knew it did. "I can't get through to her. Why can't she see marrying me is the best thing for all of us?"

"Is it?"

Sawyer stared at his mother. "Are you kidding me? Do you want my baby to disappear from our lives?"

"Of course I don't want that. I'm only wondering how much you've prayed about it. Are you seeking God's will?"

"How could God's will be different? That makes no sense."

Mom offered a sad smile. "That's what I'm talking about."

"Hit me with your deep meaning." He widened his stance and crossed his arms over his chest. "Pretend I'm too stupid to figure out what you mean."

Because he was.

CHAPTER 13

C *ome for Thanksgiving dinner? We haven't seen you for a while.*

Anna stared at the text from her uncle, her mind whirling. It would never do, though. Gloria had assumed Anna would stay at Eaglecrest, and Anna wasn't up for answering the questions that would come if she bowed out at this late notice. Especially if they knew where she was going instead. Not after Cheri's confrontation a couple of weeks back.

Uncle Paul meant well, mostly. Aunt Krissy... who knew with her? Like her sister, she spent far too much time imbibing. *I'm sorry. I won't be able to make it. I appreciate the invitation, though!*

Aw, come on. Dillon will be home from Missoula for the weekend. Maybe he'll get to see his kid.

All the more reason she couldn't go. If Sawyer or one of his brothers figured out Anna's relationship to the Scarborough family, she'd be lucky to be out on her ear. The adoption papers would never be signed. She'd be stuck as a single mother, destined to follow in her mother's tottering footsteps. Her fingers trembled as she texted back. *I can't. And it would be best if you didn't contact me again.*

No promises. Wink.

Her uncle might not be the kind of man who interfered all the time, but trusting him to keep this secret seemed a big stretch. If only Sawyer had just signed the papers in October. Then she wouldn't have to worry about him discovering her family tree.

Tell Dillon to leave me alone, too.

LOL tell him yourself.

She already had but might need to repeat it, since Uncle Paul thought this whole situation was a big joke. He couldn't wait for the Delgados to figure out they'd been had once again. Oh, not that he condoned Dillon's treatment of Cheri, exactly, but he'd still found the fallout mildly amusing.

At least this text had come while Anna had been at the apartment. She needed to make absolutely certain she never left her phone where anyone else could find it. Like Sawyer.

She shuddered.

He was already a coiled spring. His frustration had come through loud and clear a few days ago, and she'd done her best to steer clear of him since.

Thankfully — for Anna — one of the cows had fallen ill and several others had come down with whatever afflicted it. Sawyer and his dad had been out in the barns at all hours, and Lauren Carmichael, the veterinarian, had made several visits.

His gaze sizzled Anna's skin over lunch. She'd started taking leftovers out to the apartment for supper... and indulging in so much tutti-frutti ice cream she was going to need another trip to town soon to stock up.

Evenings were long and lonely. Dr. Miller had recommended prenatal classes — as if — so she'd read some articles and watched a few videos online. Everyone assumed the baby's father would be right there, coaching the mother through childbirth.

Anna didn't want to think about sharing that with Sawyer.

Maybe when she returned to Bozeman with the signed papers and had selected the baby's parents, they'd want to coach the birth. Did she want to go through the experience with strangers?

Not at all, but she wanted her mother even less. Mom and her sister, Krissy, were two peas in a pod like their mother had been before them.

Alcohol was not the answer to life's problems. The curse ended with Anna, even though her mom kept mumbling about the sins of the mothers being visited on their children.

That was from Shakespeare, right? Anna had a vague memory of *The Merchant of Venice* from junior English class, mostly because some of the parents had challenged the lit department as to whether such anti-Semitic material was appropriate for vulnerable students. She'd paid better attention in class than she might have otherwise, looking for the divisive parts, but that only made her remember the quote better.

Better, but not good enough for the details. There was some argument in the play about whether it was the sins of the fathers or of the mothers, wasn't there?

Ten years later, and she couldn't remember the final conclusion to the drama. She brought up a search on her phone and stared. Yes, one of the results featured Shakespeare's well-known play, but the origin of the quote was the Bible?

Anna's heart sank. If that were true, there really was no hope. The words seemed to be in the Bible in several places. She tapped one of the references, and Jeremiah 32:17-18 popped up.

Ah, Sovereign Lord, you have made the heavens and the earth by your great power and outstretched arm. Nothing is too hard for you. You show love to thousands but bring the punishment for the parents' sin into the laps of their children after them. Great and mighty God, whose name is the Lord Almighty.

It was worse than she'd thought. Her mom and aunt were being punished for their mother's sins. And now she was chastised because of *her* mother. No wonder Dillon was such a mess. Just look at Aunt Krissy.

There was no hope for the human race at all. Doom and gloom deepened everywhere.

The baby booted her soundly in the bladder.

Anna covered the spot on her belly. Would this child escape the curse by being adopted by someone else? Or would the genetics show, regardless?

"God?" she whispered. "This is too hard for me. Back

in September I thought there was some peace. Some hope. I thought You loved me. Cared about the situation. Was I wrong?"

At the least, she'd thought she'd find atonement by giving a deserving couple their dream come true. She'd expected to partition herself. The baby would grow in one area, where her emotions wouldn't touch it. She'd keep it separate from her own essence.

But it was hard not to acknowledge the tiny being. She'd asked the ultrasound tech to avert the monitor, but that hadn't kept the transducer's pressure on her skin from coolly registering reality.

Her old jeans were in full gap mode, and the stretchy leggings Sawyer had bought her were far more comfortable. Her circumference was only going to increase. The baby was going to grow more active. The emotional wall she'd strived to build faltered with every flutter.

How could she give this child up? But how could she not, when she could protect it from the generational curse?

THE COUGH that had plagued dozens of cows had finally been quelled. Sawyer and his brothers had quarantined the affected animals at the first sign of distress. No doubt that was the only reason it hadn't spread through the entire herd.

He couldn't even imagine the panic that would have induced. Even now, he felt like he could hardly breathe himself. His eyes watered and his throat itched in solidarity with the cattle. Every muscle in his body ached.

"It's not inter-species transferable." Lauren Carmichael looked as exhausted as he felt. "So whatever you're coming down with isn't from them."

Sawyer stared at the veterinarian dully. He was coming down with something? That would explain how terrible he felt. He glanced toward his brothers, who were leaning on the corral fence, deep in conversation, just starting their shift.

Like Sawyer, Dad had hauled the night shift riding herd, but he'd already gone inside to drop in bed. That's where Sawyer needed to be. Max had already led Debonair away.

"Thanks. For everything." He thumbed toward the recovering animals.

She grinned. "The bill will be in the mail."

He managed a chuckle. "You've earned your pay."

"I'll give Kade and Trevor final instructions. You go on. Sleep for a week. You look like you need it."

"Yeah." He felt like he needed it, too. The plowed farmyard seemed particularly uneven as he stumbled across it then up the back steps and into the entry.

Mom appeared in the kitchen door, her brow furrowing as she took him in. "Sawyer? Are you all right?"

"Coming down with something," he mumbled.

She came closer and pressed her hand to his forehead. "You're burning up. You hungry? I'll give you a few minutes to get settled in bed and I'll bring you something."

Hungry? He shook his head.

"Tea then. And some broth."

"Broth?" he repeated.

"And tea." Mom lifted a hand. "No argument, son. I'll stand over you while you drink it if I need to."

Sawyer sagged to the bench and pried off his cowboy boots. He shed his jacket, and his mom reached to hang it up. She swiped the hat off his head, while she was at it. Thankfully, the back stairs were only a few feet away with his bedroom at the head of them. He could make it that much farther.

He gave a longing look toward the shower in his ensuite. That would warm him up, wouldn't it? But staying upright that long would have to wait until he'd slept. Somehow, he managed to don flannel pajama pants and a Henley before crawling beneath his king-sized down comforter.

Ahh. Bliss.

Mom's voice followed a light tap at the door. "Ready in there?" At his affirmative grunt, she pushed into the room carrying a tray, which she set on his nightstand. "Broth first. Careful, it's hot."

Home-canned chicken broth had always been his mother's cure for what ailed any of them. Good to see some things hadn't changed in the years he'd been away. Sawyer elbowed himself up on his pillow, accepted the thermal mug, then took a sip. The robust flavors of chicken, garlic, and ginger seeped into his mouth. "Thanks."

"You look done in." Mom pulled a chair to his bedside. "But you can't succumb to this bug, all right? It's just a few days until Thanksgiving. We've not only got our entire family coming for turkey dinner, but also Cheri's grandparents and Denae's dad and stepmom. You won't want to miss a minute of it."

They didn't matter a speck to him. It was time with Anna he didn't want to miss out on. He was pretty sure she was avoiding him, but it had been hard to tell with as much time as he'd spent nursing cattle. She wouldn't be able to skip Thanksgiving dinner.

"And then we'll get Christmas decorations up." Mom grinned at him. "I can't tell you how thrilled I am that you're home for the entire season this year. I've sure missed having you around."

"Sounds... busy." Generally, he liked busy. Right now, it all seemed too much pressure. He took a few more swallows. The savory liquid soothed his scratchy throat.

"Here, have some chamomile tea." She pulled one mug from his listless hand and replaced it with the other. "On Friday we can all go out in the forest and haul in some spruce trees. Cheri and Denae have both put in an order for two. We need three. Oh, and one for Anna's apartment." Mom eyed him. "Do you think she'll want one?"

How should he know? She ran hot and cold with everything else. Other than remaining obstinate about not marrying him, of course. Sawyer tried to shrug, but barely managed a twitch. He took another sip of the tea and set it down with shaky hands.

"Poor baby," his mother said lightly. She reached up and tugged the heavy drapery over the nearest window, then rounded the bed and did the same on the other side. She pressed her fingers to her lips then patted his cheek. "Sleep well. I'll pray you awaken rested and healthy."

When the door closed behind her, Sawyer stared up at the lazily circling ceiling fan just visible in the dim light.

Would Ace ever awaken rested and healthy? Not likely. Last Sawyer had heard from Adam, brain activity had diminished. The thought of his vibrant friend slowly losing his grip on life crushed Sawyer's heart every time he thought of it. Mostly he kept too busy to think.

A man never knew when his time would be up. Ace's kid would never know the good, solid man who'd sired him. Sure, rough around the edges, but as honest as the day was long.

Sawyer's kid? That was going to be different. If Anna refused to marry him, he'd have to take a page from his brother's book and raise the child himself. Oh, he wasn't a saint like Kade, who'd taken on someone else's infant.

The baby Anna carried was Sawyer's flesh and blood. He'd likely be the only child Sawyer ever fathered if Anna vanished, because Sawyer couldn't imagine loving another woman the way he was coming to love her.

He held onto the thought, willing it to triumph over memories of Ace, as he drifted off to sleep.

CHAPTER 14

Anna glanced around the great room and the kitchen from the breakfast room, but Sawyer was nowhere to be seen. His brothers were deep in conversation while the little boys played with the toy ranch set near the hearth.

"Looking for Sawyer?" Cheri elbowed Anna lightly. "He's recuperating from the man flu. You've heard of it, I'm sure. It's the most incapacitating disease in the known world. Rumors of his imminent death have not been exaggerated."

Denae rolled her eyes. "Oh, you. He's already feeling much better than he was earlier this week. I'm just glad *I* didn't have to take care of sick cattle for three nights straight."

"That, too." Cheri grinned. "But there really isn't anything more pathetic than a sick cowboy. Don't tell me Trevor isn't that bad."

"He hasn't come down with anything since the

wedding, so I'm reserving judgment." Denae glanced between them. "I saw Sawyer a few hours ago, and he's feeling a lot better. He'll be coming downstairs for dinner."

"Can't keep a good man down." Cheri chuckled. "Or should I say, can't keep a Delgado man away from food for long. Seriously, though, I'm glad he's doing better. Being sick is no fun."

Anna had no desire to get the flu. She wouldn't let him get close enough to infect her, and not just to protect her health or the baby's. Distance was the best thing, all around. She had her emotions to think of, too. She kept being weak and hormonal and succumbing to Sawyer's strong yet gentle arms, but that needed to stop. Would stop. Had already stopped.

"Your mom drove back to Oregon for Thanksgiving?"

She startled then realized Cheri asked Denae, not her. Who knew what her own mother was doing for Thanksgiving? So long as she hadn't decided to join her sister in Saddle Springs and accidentally — or on purpose — tell the world about Anna's relationships.

"Yes, Gloria invited her to Eaglecrest, but the boys couldn't get time off from the resort. Mom didn't want to leave them alone over the holiday weekend, even though they'll be working a good part of the time."

Anna had seen Denae's younger half-brothers at the wedding, not that she'd been paying much attention to the bumbling ushers. Her eyes had been filled with the groom's hunky, flirtatious youngest brother. And look where that had gotten her. No one to blame but herself.

How come Cheri was being so nice today, like she

hadn't jabbed Anna in the baby gut last week? She might have let the topic go, but Anna couldn't help but be wary around her after that. She was wary of everyone at the moment. It was exhausting, and the end of the year seemed lost in the vague and distant future.

Would Sawyer follow through and sign the papers as he'd promised? Anna had no reason to believe he'd back out, but it wasn't going to come easily, and it definitely wasn't coming early. He wasn't done trying to convince her to marry him.

Could she be happy with him while holding her secrets forever? Except secrets had a way of leaking out. No, she had to hold on until she got Sawyer's signature on the adoption paperwork. Cheri and Kade were definitely not an option. She needed total strangers.

Anna forced her thoughts back to the moment.

Ruthie ruled the kitchen, directing Russ as he lifted the sizzling golden turkey from the wall oven. She jabbed a temperature probe into the thigh. The rich aroma of the roasting meat swirled through the space, and Anna's stomach growled in response.

She'd never been so hungry in her life as since becoming pregnant. Anna stepped around Denae. "Can I do anything to help with dinner?"

"No, no." Ruthie flapped her apron toward her. "Everything is under control. Even the table is set. You go ahead and relax. Russ, could you cover the turkey with foil? It needs to rest a bit."

Russ winked at Anna but did as he was told.

The doorbell rang, and Denae and Cheri headed for the foyer.

Anna heard them greet the visitors. Cheri's grandparents still lived on Paradise Creek Ranch halfway down River Road, not far from the new house on the bluff where Cheri and Kade and their family lived. They'd hired a woman who acted as a nurse and companion to the older couple, but Dottie had the weekend off to visit family in Boise.

A man's laughter sounded from the foyer. That was definitely not Cheri's grandfather, so Denae's dad and his wife had also arrived from Missoula.

She wished she could afford to get Mr. Archibald's legal advice on the adoption paperwork. Maybe the woman at the agency had overstated the case and she could release the baby for adoption without Sawyer's signature. But his words that October night in the fairgrounds still stopped her cold. *Don't even try to test me. I'll block you. I promise.*

Anna believed him. She'd walked right into that one. She should never have assumed he'd remained the same easy guy she'd slept with in June.

He was anything but.

A whisper from the back stairs compelled her to turn.

Sawyer. His skin was paler than usual and his plaid flannel shirt untucked over his jeans, but he was upright. Upright was good. His intense gaze zeroed in on hers. "Hey."

She managed an awkward smile. She should stop staring at him. She should figure out once and for all how to keep her distance and wait out the remainder of the year, but his dark eyes caught her every time. "You look like you're feeling better."

He nodded. "How are you?" He flicked a glance at her belly. "How's our baby doing?"

"*The* baby." Her response was automatic by now. Good thing, because the distancing word became harder to pull to the forefront with every flip of the growing fetus.

Sawyer quirked a grin. "*My* baby."

They could argue this point for hours, and she'd never win because he was just that much more obstinate than her.

"Hey, hon, you're looking better."

Anna felt the tension seep away as Gloria hurried past and gave her strapping son a hug.

His arms came around his mom for a second, and he patted her back. "Feeling better, too."

"Good. It's been long enough that you won't be contagious anymore. Our guests have arrived, if you'd like to head into the great room and be sociable for a few minutes. Ruthie, Dad, and I will finish getting the meal on the table."

Sawyer gestured to the doorway. "After you."

Great. Now they were arriving like a couple, not that it probably mattered what the visitors thought. It wasn't all about her.

"Sawyer!" Denae's dad turned and gripped the cowboy's hand. "Heard you were home for good. Welcome back to Montana."

"Yes, sir. It's good to be back. Have you met Anna Winter? She's the mother of my child."

Heat shot up Anna's cheeks as the attorney turned to

her. That wording had slipped off his tongue like he'd practiced it for weeks. Still, what was a better way to introduce her to people he knew? "Good afternoon, Mr. Archibald."

"Stewy." He shook her hand firmly, his smile warm. "I believe I've seen you around Saddle Springs some."

"Yes, I worked at the Branding Iron Bar and Grill for several years."

"That would be where, then. Good food. Excellent service." He grinned as he turned back to Sawyer. "What's the latest on Ace Desjardins? Any improvement? I've been following his case with interest."

Sawyer swayed slightly, and it was all Anna could do not to support him. The guy was just off his sickbed, no matter what his mom said. It wasn't a great time to remind him of his friend's plight.

"No improvement. Just the opposite, in fact. Last I heard a few days ago, his organs were failing." Sawyer took a deep breath. "They're considering removing life support."

"Tough decision for his loved ones." Stewy shook his head. "It's a bad situation all the way around."

Anna angled her head, trying to hear the nuances. What made it worse circumstances than the obvious?

"It really is. His mother barely leaves Ace's bedside, praying hard for his recovery, and his ex..." Sawyer rubbed his forehead. "She's only ever been after the money."

"They weren't married, though, were they?"

"No. Ace didn't think they were all that serious, either. Vanessa was a buckle bunny, mostly hanging around for the glory of being seen with a winning cowboy." Sawyer grimaced. "Guess I should be thankful I wasn't at the top of the charts. Ace was."

Stewy shook his head, face skewed in disgust.

"Ace had walked away with a lot of prize money this season, and Vanessa had her eyes on that. She was seriously annoyed when he tried to break off with her. He'd refound his faith and realized kids were looking up to him as a rodeo star."

"Good for him wanting to be a better example."

"And now his legacy will be forever tainted." Sawyer's eyes narrowed. "She makes me so angry I can't even—"

His voice broke off, his jaw clenched.

Anna's heart pierced at the dark, brooding expression on his face.

Sawyer took in a sharp breath. "He'd been invited to speak to a private high school the next week, so Vanessa was pretty gleeful about dropping her bombshell that night, not long before Ace mounted Cramer."

"Trying to sabotage his ride?" Stewy stared intensely at Sawyer. "What was she going to get out of that?"

"She figured no one would want to hear his story if they knew he hadn't been practicing what he preached."

Stewy whistled. "So... blackmail?"

Anna's head swam.

"That night it was just a veiled threat, but I think she'd have gone there. I doubt Ace would have caved. He was all about owning up to his mistakes, but yeah, the high school might've retracted the speaking offer. There could have been other repercussions. We'll likely never know how it would have played out."

"And Vanessa's still angling for money?"

"You betcha. She's playing the grieving pregnant girl-friend who deserves everything. With DNA paternity tests available pre-birth now, she's been able to petition the court that her child should be Ace's heir."

"And she'd be the trustee."

"Exactly."

"So she has a vested interest in his removal from life support. That's... despicable."

Sawyer's arms crossed over his chest. "She's nothing but an opportunistic tramp. When I think of all the havoc she's caused, I wish they could pin Ace's accident on her and send her to jail for manslaughter or something."

Anna backed up a step, reaching for the wall behind her.

"Not likely possible from a legal point of view." Stewy's lips drew into a thin line as he shook his head. "But I understand your sentiments."

"Babies shouldn't be pawns in someone's games. They're real, living humans, and they deserve to be loved and protected, not used for one parent to get even with the other for an imagined slight." Sawyer glanced at Anna, his eyes deep and dark. "Or, worse yet, for money."

Her hand went to her throat. What did he know?

He thought... she had... what *did* he think? Surely, he hadn't guessed... no. He wouldn't be talking this way if he had. He'd have her shoved back up against the wall and his eyes would be drilling holes through her soul. He wouldn't hurt her. He wasn't that kind of guy. But he would certainly let her know he could if he wanted to.

Too many bodies in this room. Not enough air.

"Excuse me." Her voice came from a distance as she backed up a step. She needed out of the great room. Maybe out of the house, across the yard, to the garage apartment. Maybe she should throw her stuff in her car and leave now.

Maybe raising the poor child herself was her penance.

Another step back, but something was behind her. A short, bumbling body. Donovan? Anna stumbled, tried to regain her balance. Failed.

CHAPTER 15

S awyer stretched his hands toward Anna as she flailed backward. He might've made his living with instantaneous reactions, but this moment was stuck in slo-mo. "Anna!" He grasped her hands just before her head collided with the tile floor, barely lessening the impact.

The force of her falling body against his grip caused him to stumble forward, but at least he didn't fall on top of her. At least he'd broken her fall, if only a little.

Panic clawed at his throat as he dropped to his knees beside her. "Anna?" He swiped her hair aside.

She moaned and turned her head away.

Stewy knelt on the other side. "Are you okay?"

Anna's eyelids fluttered. "I-I think so."

Sawyer gathered her into his arms and turned to the great room. He poked his chin toward Denae and Michelle. "Anna needs the sofa."

His sister-in-law and her stepmom surged to their feet, making room. He laid Anna down, grabbed a plush throw from a nearby chair, and tucked it around her before smoothing her hair once again. "Just rest, sweetheart," he murmured. Wow, that had taken more out of his flu-weakened body than he'd expected.

"Donovan?" she whispered.

A quick glance showed the toddler swiping a toy horse from his big brother and running off with it, giggling. "He's fine. I don't think he even noticed."

"Dad!" whined Jericho. "Donny isn't playing nice."

Sawyer turned his back on his nephews and refocused on Anna. "Is the baby okay?" He rested his hand on her belly but couldn't feel movement. Not that he had before, either.

Anna pushed his hand away. "It's fine."

Right, she probably thought he was being too familiar in front of the extended family. What did it matter? They all knew he'd fathered her child, so touching her abdomen through her clothes and a fluffy blanket shouldn't faze anyone. Anyone but Anna.

"Does your head hurt?"

"No." She glared at him. "Stop hovering." She struggled to get her elbows under her but it didn't come easily.

Sawyer nudged her back against the cushion. "Just stay. In fact, I'll bring your plate to you here when dinner is ready."

"You don't need to."

How could he ever convince this stubborn, single-minded woman that she wasn't a chore to him? That he loved her?

He stared into her hazel eyes, willing her to see the truth

he couldn't speak. For one thing, those words were, in fact, too intimate for present company and, for another, he was afraid to say them. She'd throw them back in his face. Stomp on them. Deny them.

Sawyer's heart wasn't tough enough to handle that level of rejection. Getting through this stage in one piece was all he could deal with. Come what may, she'd hear those words before she walked away on New Year's Eve. He would put everything on the line.

Today was not that day.

THE TURKEY DINNER WAS DELICIOUS. No surprise there, since Ruthie was a talented cook. To Anna's surprise, Russ had made the pumpkin pies. Did Sawyer enjoy dabbling in the kitchen like his dad? She didn't know.

At the close of the meal, Russ invited everyone into the great room to watch the NFL game.

Kade and his wife exchanged a look then Cheri rose, folding her napkin with a grimace. "Sorry, but we have to run. Dillon's in town and wants to see Harmony."

Anna's insides froze solid, and her vision swam.

"You'll leave the boys with us, won't you?" asked Gloria. "I'll put Donovan down for his nap."

"If we may." Kade pulled to his feet, ruffling Donny's hair in the high chair. "Thanks, Mom. We should be back in two or three hours."

Cheri's grandparents also stood. Chester looked a little shaky these days. They must be getting on in years, but were still living on their own with a lot of help from the woman Delgados had hired for their care.

"Thanks for dinner." Chester nodded at Russ and Gloria. "Much obliged, but we'll be headin' for home."

"We're so glad you could come." Gloria smiled warmly. "Maybe I can wrap up some leftovers for you?"

"No, that's all right." Edith reached for her sweater. "Dottie set up our meals. We'll be jes' fine until she gets back."

"If you're sure."

Anna watched as Kade helped Cheri's grandmother with her coat while Cheri bundled Harmony into hers. Soon the five of them had left the house, and Gloria lifted a sleepy Donovan from the high chair. The little guy nestled against his grandmother. Gloria's gaze met Anna's across the table.

She swallowed hard. Gloria would be happy to be that grandma for Sawyer's baby — *the* baby — too. She didn't differentiate between any of Kade and Cheri's kids, even though Donovan was the only one of the three with Delgado blood.

If only.

Life was full of those, but Anna figured she had more than her fair share. The current one? If only Dillon would keep his mouth shut about his relationship to Anna. All she really didn't need was for him to spill the beans before she had Sawyer's name scrawled on that form.

"Do you do any family law?"

Anna froze at Sawyer's casual question to Stewy

Archibald. Maybe Dillon sharing her secret wasn't the only way this day could get worse.

Sawyer hadn't missed the tension radiating off Anna as he pulled out her chair. He gripped her hand and led her to the great room, walking beside Stewy while Michelle remained, chatting with his mom. If he loosened his clasp, she'd disappear... unless she were too curious to run away.

"Not really," Stewy replied. "Our practice handles criminal law. I mean, I've got a good grasp of the basics, but it's not my specialty."

"I've got a couple of questions."

It definitely wasn't Sawyer's imagination that Anna jerked against his hand, but he nudged her onto the end of the sofa and sat close beside her, keeping a firm grip.

"Go for it." Stewy settled into the nearby armchair. "You've met Denae's best friend, Sadie Santoro. She's a family law attorney in Spokane, which also isn't much help legally since she's not licensed in Montana. But she might be able to offer some insights if I can't."

Sawyer recalled the woman who'd been Denae's matron-of-honor. Sadly, she likely remembered him as the annoying playboy he'd been back in June and would think his present situation served him right. Which it kind of did.

He squeezed Anna's hand but didn't look at her. "The thing is, Anna and I are at a bit of an impasse. She'd like to put our baby up for adoption, and I don't want that."

Anna inhaled unsteadily.

Stewy sharpened his gaze and steepled his hands. "I see."

"I want to marry her, but she refuses." He didn't release Anna's hand though it pulled strongly. "The other alternatives I see are that either she raises the baby on her own... or I do. Are we missing an option?"

"Sawyer," she hissed under her breath.

"That covers the possibilities." Stewy looked between them. "Although an open adoption could allow a variation on that front."

"No." Anna's voice was a little stronger. "Why are we having this discussion? There's only one right answer."

"Kade and Cheri offered to adopt, but I agree with Anna. It doesn't seem like a good solution." It would kill him to watch his child call Kade *Dad*.

"It wouldn't have to be a family member. Couples who are currently strangers to you both might be willing to consider allowing some access. I believe it's quite common in recent years."

"No." Anna yanked her hand out of his. "I want a standard closed adoption."

The attorney studied her. "Those are very rare anymore, and usually not considered to be in the child's best interest."

"That's what I thought." Sawyer tried to recapture her hand, but she glared at him and tucked it in her armpit. At least she hadn't flounced out of the room.

"The level of access can vary greatly, though," the attorney continued. "You can potentially negotiate areas like meeting and choosing the adoptive parents yourself, annual photos and updates, or time spent with the child at certain intervals." He shrugged. "Nearly everything is negotiable, really."

"What happens when the two parents don't agree? I understand the mother cannot place the baby without the father's consent in Montana." That tidbit had come from another competitor who'd found himself in a similar situation a couple of years ago.

Against his shoulder, Anna stiffened.

"I believe that's true, unless the father is unknown. Although, like I said, family law is not my specialty."

Doubts of Anna's baby's parentage still niggled at the back of Sawyer's mind. Vanessa had managed to prove the baby she carried was Ace's, though. They'd swabbed Ace's mouth for a DNA sample even in his unconscious state. Sawyer would give his up willingly.

But what if the baby proved not to be his, after all? Anna seemed to have no doubts, but... if she'd slept with Sawyer as willingly as she had back in June, how could he be certain she hadn't had other lovers? Like Dillon. Man, that would burn big time. How good an actor was she? Because she'd seemed genuinely horrified when Sawyer had accused her.

What if all this was a lie to get something out of him? But she wouldn't be seeking adoption if what she really wanted was child support.

No matter how many times his brain spiraled in circles, he couldn't make sense of her reluctance.

"Another alternative is for the two of you to share custody. You'd agree on time frames and so forth. That's how Denae's mother and I handled things in her childhood. Denae spent the school year with Lisa in Oregon and summers with me. We had to talk to each other more than I would have liked at times. It was especially awkward after Michelle and I got married, but it was a small price for staying in my daughter's life."

Sawyer hadn't considered that.

"No." Anna surged to her feet and crossed her arms over her chest. "It's adoption or—" She pressed her lips together.

The stance showcased her baby bulge. Sawyer couldn't help staring. His child. His baby. This little life was not going to some stranger somewhere.

"Or what?" asked Stewy.

She glared at Sawyer then at the attorney. "Or nothing. That's the only option."

It was time to man up. "Or I'll raise our baby myself."

Anna pivoted to stare down at him. "You can't."

"Why not? Kade did it and survived."

There'd been no biological reason for his brother to accept responsibility for Daniela's baby. Kade was just that kind of guy, always trying to lend a helping hand to others. He'd given up all hope of reconciling with Cheri at that point in his life, but instead of becoming bitter, he'd chosen to love a dying woman and her baby. Sawyer might call him Saint Kade in teasing, but it was close to reality.

Anna shook her head. "You don't know what you're talking about."

Sawyer fought the urge to shoot to his feet, tower over her, and take command of this conversation. She'd block him out. She'd run. If the only way to make her listen was to let her stand alone, he'd do it.

He'd do anything.

He angled his head and looked up at her. "What don't I know? If the baby is mine, he's mine, and I'm not giving him away." There, that gave her two things to challenge. *Choose one.*

"You don't know it's a boy. Stop talking like that."

That's the argument she picked? He shrugged. "I'd love my daughter just as much." *His daughter.* Could it be? That would be a lot tougher. What did he know about hair bows and frilly dresses and fairy princesses? Well, he'd figure it out. The baby better be a boy, though. He could deal with that.

"Sawyer—" She pinched her lips together.

He spared a glance for the attorney, who sat watching the spectacle intensely. Several family members had gathered at the other end of the great room around the TV above the fireplace. If they were listening, so be it.

Sawyer had no secrets. Did Anna? He cocked his eyebrows at her. "I'm ready to do a paternity test to prove I have parental rights."

She inhaled sharply.

It was a gamble. There'd be no going back from the results for either of them. If Sawyer was the father, he'd hold firm, but what if he wasn't? What if the swab proved otherwise?

Could he let Anna and the baby disappear from his life?

CHAPTER 16

No doubt Sawyer was having the time of his life with Anna clinging to his waist. He revved the snowmobile and carved a swath in the deep snow, dragging a long sled behind them. Ahead of them, Harmony and Jericho screamed and waved from the sled behind their parents' machine. Two more snowmobiles rounded out the group.

If only Anna could have stayed home, but no. It had been expected she'd be delighted to come on a family excursion to cut trees for everyone's houses. Sawyer assumed she wanted a tree for the garage apartment. With borrowed ornaments? Not hardly.

The crisp air bit her nose, but the sunshine was glorious as it sparkled off the fresh snow. It hadn't snowed yet down in Saddle Springs, but it lay thick this high up in the mountains. It was true she'd spent too much time indoors since the first snowfall when they'd gone to Cheri and Kade's.

Anna couldn't trust Cheri. Not when she spent time

with Dillon since they shared a daughter. Not when Cheri was eager to adopt Anna's baby. *The* baby. If only Cheri would keep from getting overly curious or letting the wrong things slip when she was around the Scarboroughs.

Up ahead, Denae pointed to the left, and Trevor slowed their snowmobile. Russ and Gloria idled up beside them. The foursome conferred then powered off both machines before reaching for the snowshoes everyone had packed along.

Anna didn't want to snowshoe. She didn't want a Christmas tree. She just wanted all this to be over, but there were still five weeks to go. Oh, and then a few more months.

Though your sins are like scarlet, they shall be as white as snow: though they are red as crimson, they shall be like wool.

That was in the Bible somewhere, wasn't it? A pang of guilt stabbed Anna. She'd accepted Jesus a few months back, but she hadn't spent a lot of time digging into the Bible. Everything seemed on hold. It felt like she had to get through this season on her own and then she'd be good enough. But hadn't Jesus covered her sin? Yeah, but...

She'd have to tell Sawyer everything. And then he'd hate her... but he would, anyway. Why not ensure it? It wasn't like she expected a happy ending from all this.

Sawyer parked beside the others and lifted off his helmet as he turned to grin at her. "Ready?"

No? But he never heard her words. She'd tried to insist on staying back at the ranch, but she'd suddenly found herself wearing a parka with a helmet on her head. Saying no to Sawyer Delgado was like washing a fish by swishing it in the ocean. It had no impact.

On the other hand, Sawyer knelt in the snow and strapped the snowshoe harnesses around her boots. Yes, without asking, but he'd surmised correctly that she didn't know how. Also that it was getting more difficult to reach her feet.

She sat on the machine while he buckled into his own snowshoes. Then he rose and gave a few stamps before flashing her a grin and reaching for her hands.

It wasn't quite the same as just walking, since the snowshoes widened her stance. From what she'd heard, waddling was likely in her future, anyway. She just got to practice early, thankfully with ski poles to help with balance. Yay.

"Follow my footsteps when you can," he instructed. "That will make it a bit easier. But holler if you see a tree you think you'd like, and we'll take a closer look."

Not far away, Kade lifted a baby carrier to his back with Cheri's help. Donovan shouted with glee while his big brother and sister clomped around in their kid-sized snowshoes.

Anna's spirits rose. It really was beautiful. The air, crisp and clean. The vista, pristine. Magnificent.

White as snow. Those Bible words really meant something, but how did they stack up to the bit about the sins of the fathers? They couldn't both be true, could they? Right now, with thick layers of glistening whiteness obscuring most of the landscape and weighing heavily on the evergreens, it was easy to believe God's love could cover everything. Yet, wouldn't the ugliness be revealed again, later, when the snow melted? Decomposing logs, broken branches, pits to stumble in?

Gloria plodded over to a smallish tree and poked it with her ski pole. Snow cascaded off, revealing gapping branches shorter on one side. "Not this one!" she hollered with a laugh.

"It's cute!" yelled Harmony. "I want it."

"I don't think so." Cheri chuckled. "We're looking for something more symmetrical. That means the same from every angle. It needs to be just perfect to come home with us."

It felt like a cloud had come over the sun, though it shone as brightly as before. Wasn't that the way of it? Perfection was required. Oh, not just for the Delgados. This was only a sample of life.

Like Anna, the little tree couldn't help where its roots dug in. Couldn't help its surroundings or the conditions that marred its beauty.

"How about this one, Mama?" Jericho raced toward another tree but tripped over something hidden in the snow and face-planted. Before any of the adults could reach him, he'd pushed himself up to kneeling and shoved his knit hat on straighter. He pointed. "See it?"

Anna settled in for long hours following the Delgado crew from one tree to the next. Her thighs were already killing her. She held a vision of a steaming, candlelit bubble bath in front of her. She would have earned that respite by the time they came down off the mountain.

And maybe she'd take that awkward little tree home with her to the garage apartment. She felt a bit of an affinity with it. The stubby side could go against the window, and the rest of it wasn't so bad. It didn't deserve judgment.

Sawyer glanced over at Anna as Trevor crouched to cut a tree with the lightweight chainsaw he'd carried on his back. Tiredness shimmered off Anna in waves, and guilt stabbed him. He shouldn't have forced her to come, not in her condition.

A little grin pushed at his lips. She hated those words and had flared more than once when he'd said them.

Leaning heavily on both ski poles, she met his gaze. Her eyebrows rose slightly, like she asked a question. *How much longer?*

This was only tree five out of seven, and it had taken over an hour to get this far. But, maybe, it was enough for him and Anna. He turned to Trevor in the sudden silence as the chainsaw powered down. "I'll haul that back to the snowmobiles for you. Then, I think Anna and I are headed back to the ranch."

Her eyebrows shot all the way up as she straightened.

Yeah, definitely time.

Mom tromped closer to Anna. "You okay, hon?"

"Sure, but I'm done in." Anna offered a wan smile.

Sawyer grabbed the trunk of the downed spruce and dragged it down the path toward the river. Once there, he wrestled it into the sled on top of the others they'd cut earlier and roped them down. Then he looked for Anna.

She stood up the trail a little, head tilted to one side as she examined the short spruce they'd first rejected.

He tromped over to her. "Whatcha thinking?"

Anna glanced up at him. "This little guy would look good in the corner by the window."

"Really? This little Charlie Brown tree?" She'd cut off every offer for a tree in the garage apartment. "Why not a bushier one?"

"This one. I know it's not perfect, but neither am I."

Understanding seeped in. Sawyer set his arm across her shoulders. "Sweetheart, only God is perfect, but you're perfect for me."

"I'm not." It was only a whisper.

"You keep saying that, but I don't get it." He really didn't. So often, she seemed ready to give in but then found her backbone again. It just didn't make sense. They'd started off on the wrong foot, but hadn't anything he'd done to prove his devotion to her stuck, even a little?

Anna shifted sideways. "Would you cut it, please?"

Something had happened to Charlie Brown's tree when it was wrapped in Linus's blanket. When it was shown love. Maybe, just maybe, this little tree could help cause a transformation, too.

"Sure." Sawyer trudged back to the snowmobile toolbox for an axe. It didn't take many swings to slice through the thin trunk. He'd probably have to get creative with a tree stand since their trees were usually more robust, but he'd figure it out.

Anna grabbed the tree and pulled it toward the sled. She seemed to be doing okay, so he let her, but he hoisted it on top of the others and retied the ropes. By the time he'd finished, she'd managed to get her snowshoes undone. He tucked them in the sled with his own, then started the snowmobile and turned it back down the mountain.

An affinity with a Charlie Brown tree. That opened a larger window to her soul than she'd offered any other time, but he wasn't sure what to do with it. Why did she feel so unloved and unwanted?

He'd only visited Saddle Springs occasionally in the years she'd worked at the Branding Iron. He knew she'd hung out with Sabrina from Shear Expressions, but surely, she had other friends? Yet, as far as he knew, no one had made an overture in the past five weeks... other than Dillon. He frowned. There was a connection there, but what kind?

She'd mentioned coming to faith, but it seemed to bring her little joy. She'd resisted going down to Springs of Living Water Church with the family on Sundays. Sawyer hadn't been a good example there, either. Snow had kept them home last week, then he'd been sick, but those excuses didn't work for every week.

If he wanted to marry her and make a home together — and he did — he needed to step up and be a spiritual leader. Which meant he needed to dig deeper in the Word himself and come to grips with God's plan for him.

Mom had challenged him about that on several occasions. He'd grabbed onto what made sense to him and done his best to push that scenario to its logical outcome. The one he wanted. The one that was obviously right.

Yet there was something tender and wounded in Anna's spirit. Her healing had to come ahead of his ironclad will.

But, if he loosened his grip, even a little, wouldn't she bolt? This was bigger than him, bigger than her. A baby's life and entire future hung in the balance. *Their* baby.

But was the situation bigger than God?

He wrestled with it all the way down the riverside trail and was still deep in thought when he parked the snowmobile near the garage and helped Anna off the seat. "You okay?" he asked softly, searching her face.

She grimaced and didn't meet his eyes. "I'm pretty sore. I think there's a bubble bath with my name on it."

Sawyer brushed strands of hair from her face. "I didn't mean to hurt you." She could take that any way she liked. All of them were true.

"I know." Anna backed up a step, breaking contact.

"I'll set your tree in the garage for now so the rest of the snow can melt off. We'll put it up tomorrow?"

"Sure." Another step backward.

"Did you bring any lights or ornaments? If not, I can find some." An idea began to form.

Anna sighed. "I don't have any, but I don't need much. Maybe I'll make a few."

"I can help."

This time she met his eyes for a brief second as she let out a frustrated huff.

"What? You don't think I can handle a pair of scissors or a glue gun?" Not that he knew what she was thinking of creating, but how hard could it be?

"I'm sure you can. There's nothing you can't do." And with that, she pivoted for the side door and let herself in.

He watched through the window as she slowly mounted the steps and disappeared at the top.

Just a few days ago he'd have had a smart comeback for her obvious confidence in his abilities. Now, the frustration in her voice didn't sound nearly as endearing.

A Charlie Brown tree. He was going to have to pull up that old special on his phone and look beneath the surface while he watched it.

And, yes, pray. Because his way through this mess wasn't working. It was time for God to come through in a big way, because Sawyer Delgado had about reached his limit.

CHAPTER 17

Sawyer clomped up the garage stairs with a coil of rope over his shoulder and a large box in his hands. What was Anna going to think of his finds? Guess he'd soon find out.

She stood by the table, her face curious. "Where's the tree?"

"I'll bring it up in a minute." He set the box on the island counter. "I found a few things from my childhood. They seemed to suit the smaller tree."

"Beggars can't be choosers," she muttered.

"Hey, now. You haven't seen my treasures yet." He unfolded the cardboard flaps.

"I see a rope that probably got dragged through manure on its last outing."

"It's new! I was thinking it would make a nice garland. Do you have a better idea?"

She made a show of zipping her lips.

Sawyer pulled out a red child-size cowboy hat. "I loved

this thing. Wore it all day, every day for a couple of years. And then..."

"Then your head swelled out of it."

"Uh, yeah. But it would work as a topper instead of a star, wouldn't it?"

Anna angled her head and squinted at the hat. "Maybe? What else do you have in there?"

He pumped his fist. "I'm the winner!"

"Not so fast, cowboy. All I'm admitting is that I don't have any better ideas at the moment, and I don't feel like making a trip to town just for a few ornaments."

Sawyer would take progress where he could get it. "A string of white lights." He set them on the counter. "A stack of red bandanas that used to be my grandfather's."

She rolled her eyes. "What on earth would I do with those?"

He lifted a softball out of the box with one hand and a roll of twine with the other. Raised his eyebrows at her. Waited.

"You seriously have a plan for that junk? With apologies to your grandfather."

"Yup." He set the ball in the middle of a bandana and gathered the loose edges. "Now to tie it. Like so." He pulled out his sheath knife, cut a length of twine, tied off the bandana, and held it up. "Pretty good, huh?"

"I'm impressed." Though it seemed to pain her to admit as much.

Sawyer waggled his eyebrows at her. "There are more brilliant ideas where those came from."

Anna pulled the cardboard box to her side of the

counter and peered in. "What's this?" She lifted a stack of small plastic frames shaped like horseshoes.

He held his breath as she laid them out in a row, her face pensive. "You and your brothers?"

"Yeah."

"You were cute."

"I know." He managed not to add, *our baby will be, too.*

"Like I said before about the swelled head. It started early."

"I deserved that. I've always been too big for my britches. Keeping up with Trevor and Kade took a lot of effort when I was the runt."

Anna looked over at him. "Why did you get into rodeo?"

He shrugged. "Mostly because I was better at it than they were."

"Because you thought you were invincible."

"For a long time, I did think that." Sawyer held her gaze. "Although you don't get to pro levels without getting bucked off a billion times. I've had more concussions and broken bones than I can rightly recall."

"Why? I don't get it."

"Testosterone overload."

Pink warmed her cheeks, and she looked back down at the row of little frames, touching one lightly.

He rounded the island and came up beside her. "My ego and my hot blood has gotten me in a lot of trouble over the years, but Ace's accident taught me something. Hopefully a lot of things. I'm not the same man I was in June."

Anna bit her lip but didn't look up. "I've noticed."

"I'd like to think I'm a better person now. God's forgiven me for running my own way for so long. I took advantage of you, and I'm sorry. Forgive me?"

"I didn't exactly play hard to get."

He turned her toward him, his hand cradling her cheek. "Forgive me?"

"Sawyer, don't..."

"It's a simple question, sweetheart. Can you forgive me?"

Anna backed up, and his hand fell away. "It's not that easy."

"Why can't it be?" What on earth was holding her back? How could he crumble her crazy barriers? "I wronged you. I get that, and I'm truly sorry. But I've wronged Jesus more. Yet He's tossed my sins as far from His sight as the east is from the west. Have you ever thought about that? How far east do you need to go to arrive at west? It's impossible."

Anna closed her eyes and swayed slightly. She took a deep breath and looked at him with a tortured gaze. "I know everything you're doing is designed to break me down. You have this idealistic vision in your mind. Don't you get it? It's not real. It's like you're riding a unicorn instead of your horse, making daisy chains under a rainbow sky."

His mouth gaped, and he snapped it shut. "A unicorn? That's what you get out of all this? That I'm on some fairy planet my eight-year-old niece dreamed up?"

"I'm not that perfect, Sawyer. If you only knew—" Tears welled in her eyes as she turned away.

"Sweetheart."

"Don't." Her shoulders trembled.

He stepped closer and cupped her shoulders, but she twisted away and ran down the short hallway. Her bedroom door slammed behind her.

Sawyer hadn't been this afraid since he'd dropped onto that bronc's back after Ace's unmoving body had been hauled off on a stretcher. He'd walked away from his career, but he couldn't walk away from Anna.

He turned to look at the row of horseshoe frames, at the little boy grinning out at the camera. That kid had grown to think he had the world by the tail. He didn't need God. Like the fantasy in Anna's accusation, he'd set off to seek his fortune with nary a glance over his shoulder.

His chosen lifestyle hadn't left much room for faith, and God had quickly become an inconvenience pushed into a corner. Forgotten, but never completely, because how could he wipe from his memory the joy and peace he'd had as a child?

He crossed into the living room, took a seat, and shoved his fingers through his hair. Half the time he'd promised her still lay ahead of them. Promised her? More like bullied her.

Sawyer shook his head. Wow, he'd sure bungled this whole situation, starting in June and right on through November. Not that he should have signed his baby away. Never that. But he'd been so cocksure she'd be bowled over by his charm that she'd agree to marry him and solve all their problems. He'd be happy; she'd be happy; their baby, also happy, would grow up with both parents.

What if that didn't happen?

God! Sawyer's heart tore in two. *How could this not be Your will?*

Hadn't he always believed that all he needed to do was pray, and God's will would be accomplished? That verse... where was it again? In the gospels somewhere. *Ask and it will be given to you; seek and you will find; knock and the door will be opened to you. For everyone who asks receives; the one who seeks finds; and to the one who knocks, the door will be opened.*

Slam dunk.

Only not. Because then he remembered Proverbs. *Trust in the Lord with all your heart and lean not on your own understanding; in all your ways submit to him, and he will make your paths straight.*

And he'd definitely been trusting in himself more than in God. He, Sawyer John Delgado, clearly knew what was best. It was so obvious that he hadn't bothered to pray for God's will, just for the Lord to hurry up and turn Anna to the light.

He grimaced. And then they could ride off into the sunset, a perfect ending exactly like she'd accused him of.

Submitting all his ways to God sounded nerve-wracking. But he was pretty much at the end of his own devices here, and Anna was as determined as ever. Could he really place all his trust in the God of the universe?

Would he stay all night, waiting for her to come back out?

Anna lay curled on her bed, cradling her belly, tears spent. Oh, God, why did her dues have to be so high? She'd caught a glimpse of Sawyer's vision — unicorns, rainbows, and all. There was no future she'd rather step into, if only...

But the *if only* remained, a solid black barrier between her and the vision.

What was Sawyer doing out there, anyway? There were thumps and bumps then smaller sounds. Putting up that pathetic little tree? She'd asked for it on a whim, mostly because Gloria and Cheri had laughed at it. She didn't even want a Christmas tree.

The teakettle whistled.

Oh, man. That cowboy was settling in for a long stay. She needed to use the restroom, and that meant crossing the hallway. She couldn't out-wait him, but she could put it off a bit longer.

A light tap sounded on her bedroom door. "Anna? I made you a cup of tea. Do you want it in there, or do you want to see your tree?"

God, why does he have to be so perfect?

There was no answer, of course. And he wasn't, not really... but far too close. Perfect for Anna. If only.

"I'll be out in a minute."

"Okay."

She hauled a wisp of fortitude from the depth of her being, swung her legs over the side of the bed, and turned on the lamp. Ugh, her hair was a mess and her face blotchy. She should go out there and let Sawyer see what he'd be in for if she married him.

Instead, she bolted across to the bathroom and fixed

what she could before heading down the short hallway. She stopped at the end and stared at the awkward tree in the corner. He'd strung it with white lights and the rope and crowned it with the red cowboy hat. Bandana-wrapped balls hung from twine bows, and the dozen horseshoe frames filled in much of the empty space.

There were several ornaments she didn't remember seeing in the box, and moving forward for a closer look seemed easier than acknowledging the tall cowboy watching her from beside the kitchen island. She lifted a porcelain rocking horse engraved with *Baby's First Christmas*. The other side said *Sawyer John* with his birth year.

Thankfully Anna's back was to him, since tears flooded her eyes. Again.

Yeah, Sawyer was a big tough guy, but his heart was way out there on his sleeve. He might not've told her he loved her, but did he really need to say the words with a grand gesture like this one?

Her shoulders quaked as her hand dropped away from the little rocking horse. She caught a blurry glimpse of a beaded candle likely made by a preschool Sawyer, a little star cut from wood, and a reindeer made of pipe cleaners.

The baby kicked, hard, easily the most commanding movement she'd felt so far.

It was all too much. She pivoted, but she slammed straight into Sawyer's chest, his arms coming around her, likely in self-defense. And then the tears dumped out of her once again, accompanied by deep, ugly sobs.

"Hey, sweetheart." Sawyer held her close and, for once, she let him. "I didn't mean to make you cry."

Everything made her weep. The baby in her womb shared body space with the crybaby in her head.

"Did I overstep? Do you want me to take it all down?"

This was a humbler, gentler Sawyer than she'd ever known. She managed to shake her head against his chest. Man, she'd soaked that soft plaid shirt of his, and he still wasn't running. What would it take?

Maybe honesty.

He'd run from that, for sure.

Anna gathered her courage and tried to find some words. There was no easy way to say her piece, but she finally pushed away just enough to look up at Sawyer. She parted her lips to speak.

His mouth came down on hers, not as demanding as sometimes, but with sure, sweet passion.

This was definitely the last time she'd let him kiss her, but she'd need something to remember him by once the baby was safely born and adopted into its new family.

She'd tell him next time. Not tonight.

CHAPTER 18

With the onset of snow a couple of weeks ago, they'd moved all the horses down to the large stables at Trevor's place, other than the Percheron pair who were sometimes called on to pull the sleigh. Dad had bought Standing Rock Ranch from Denae's father five years back, eager for more range and hay land as well as the covered riding arena. Keeping the horses exercised with all that dedicated space was a whole lot more fun than last time Sawyer had spent the entire winter at the ranch.

Problem was, the contained area made it hard to avoid his brothers when two of them worked the horses every afternoon. Even though Kade talked twice as much as Trevor, he usually brought the kids to ride their ponies on his days, so his attention wasn't quite as focused on Sawyer.

Trevor, on the other hand, had taken a pointed interest in his kid brother. "How are things going with Anna? We're praying for you both every day."

"Thanks. How do you think Jericho's new pony is working out?"

Trevor's eyebrows rose. "Fine. And are you changing the subject?"

Sawyer swung onto his mom's mare, Friday. "It's none of your business." He nudged her flanks, and she trotted out.

His brother was only a few steps behind him on Ebony. "That's what I used to think, too. Now I figure what happens to one Delgado happens to us all."

Perfect. It was peachy keen being the youngest, coming along when the older brothers felt justified in snooping. "Yeah, well, I'm the one who screwed up in this case, not you, so it's my problem to solve."

"Prickly like a cactus." Trevor shook his head. "That's not a sign of giving everything over to God."

"I'm honestly working on that part."

"I know. Have I told you lately that I not only like you, I respect you?"

Sawyer snorted. "If we were still kids, I'd wonder what favor you wanted."

His brother grinned. "I probably deserved that."

Sawyer urged Friday into a canter. She was punchier than Debonair, but Mom got down to the arena less often than the others, so he'd taken on her mare's conditioning. The Quarter Horse loved fast turns and stops, making her and Mom into a strong cutting duo. Today, he'd use that to his advantage to dodge Trevor.

His brother stuck with him tighter than he'd have

guessed possible. "She's got good moves," Trevor said. "But you didn't answer my question."

It wasn't like Trev didn't know way too much about Sawyer's life already. That's what he got for letting it all hang out there for years. Fine. The guy wanted to hear it? Here came both barrels.

"Hard to know. Every time she loosens up a little, it doesn't take long for her to clamp right back down. It's frustrating. Like talking to a haystack, all prickly and scratchy but solid and tight."

"Any clue what seems to be the problem? From what I remember, she's never seemed to have extra money. If finances are a concern, I'd think she'd be relieved to have you take care of things."

"I'm going to pretend like you didn't just take my knees out by telling me the only reason she'd want me is to live on Easy Street."

"Well, your charm hasn't had any impact."

"Low blow." And not entirely true. She'd bawled into his chest the other night until she was spent, and he'd hoped for a day or two that things might have changed. They hadn't. If anything, she'd become more adept at avoiding him. He only had three weeks left to win her over.

"So what happens at New Year's?"

Sawyer shifted his weight back. "Whoa."

Friday's haunches dropped in a sensational sliding stop. A thing of beauty. At his signal, she regained her footing and broke into a gallop, turning tight and square at the other end. Sometimes he truly missed competitive riding.

"Yes!" hollered Trevor. "She turns on a dime, that one."

"What happens at the end of the year?" Sawyer trotted the mare toward his brother. "Wish I knew. I told her if we couldn't agree on any other course of action, I'd sign her papers."

Trev grimaced. "So she gets to decide if she concedes or not. Tough position."

"Yeah. I gave my word, and she's set on waiting me out."

"Good thing God is bigger than the situation."

"I hope so," Sawyer muttered.

Trevor spun Ebony around, staring at Sawyer from beneath his low brim. "You *hope*? Where's your faith, bro?"

"The size of a mustard seed."

"That's big enough for God to work with. You just have to get out of His way."

"I don't even know how to do that."

"Yeah, me neither."

"Well, that's a big help. Here I was waiting for your words of wisdom." Waiting for that magic wand Anna had accused him of wanting to wave. Or God's miracle. He'd take it whichever way it came.

Trevor swung off Ebony's back and led him toward the stable door. "All I know is God is in charge. And that when I start giving Him advice, He holds back until I've got nothing left. No bright ideas. No direction to turn. Blinders on my eyes, hobbles on my ankles."

"That's about where I'm at."

"Good. Then He's free to move."

Sawyer stared at his brother. "Do you have any idea how warped that sounds?"

"Yeah?" Trevor tossed a grin over his shoulder as he led Ebony away.

Sawyer nudged Friday back into a lope and stirred up the arena dirt some more. The mare followed every shift of his weight, every whisper of the reins, every word he uttered with impeccable precision. She was in her element and trusted him completely to know the results he wanted. She became his channel.

He reined her in and patted her shoulder. "You're a good girl, Friday, and smart enough to know I'm smarter than you. Guess I've got a lesson or two to learn from a horse."

ANNA LEFT Dr. Miller's office and looked up and down the street. Nope, Sawyer's big black truck was not in sight. Just as thankfully, Dillon's car wasn't, either. That had been ugly after her ultrasound.

She ducked into the real estate office next door. No one was at the front desk but, through the doorway, Paul leaned back in his chair to see who'd come in. "Anna! Long time no see. Come on back."

Another quick peek out the windows, thankfully occluded with rows of property listings, and she entered his office. "What did you want to see me for?"

"Is that any way to greet your uncle?" He patted his cheek expectantly.

He might be her uncle, but she'd pretend she didn't see that. Instead, she rounded the desk and took a seat.

"You've sure been keeping to yourself up at that ranch. Roping in that cowboy?"

"I'm still leaving at the end of the year."

Paul let his gray head fall back against the tall back of his chair dramatically. "Stubborn girl."

About time, really.

"Your mom is coming here for Christmas. She says you've blocked her calls. Really, Anna? Is that any way to treat your own mother?"

No way. Anna stared at him. "I don't want to see her. I told her that."

"Look, I've helped out all I can unless you acknowledge our relationship. So the Delgados have something against my son. He didn't treat his girlfriend right, but that's water long under the bridge. The kid is, what, eight? And growing up in the lap of luxury."

She should never have taken Paul's offer to help her find a job in Saddle Springs back then. She'd been escaping her mother and landed smack in the wake of Cheri's return with Harmony then her marriage to Kade. Paul had humored her desire to keep her distance from the family mess, and there'd never been a good reason since to openly acknowledge him, especially since Dillon had moved to Missoula. She'd walked over from her rental and visited him and Aunt Krissy occasionally during those years.

And, yes, Paul had fed her disgruntlement at the entitlement of some of the wealthier ranchers in the area. Like the Delgados. Now she'd seen how hard they worked for their money. They didn't just smile at heaven while cascades of gold coins dropped from above.

But she couldn't blame everything on Uncle Paul's attitude rubbing off on her. At least he worked for what he had, unlike Anna's mother. How could Anna ever break free? "She'll ruin everything if she comes here and contacts me. Don't let her."

Paul leaned on his desk, dark eyes narrowing at her. "She sees you as the sell-out. You had a massive prize in your grasp, and you're letting it all slip away."

Anna set her shoulders. "She ruined my life."

Her uncle dipped his chin and stared pointedly at her rounded belly. "Looks to me like you're the one who's pregnant. Maybe you've ruined your own life."

Like her mother before her. She pulled to her feet. "I'm out from under her. You tell her I'll have her arrested for theft if she contacts me."

"For theft. That's the best you can do? Because try and make it stick after all this time."

He was right. It would be a lame attempt, but what else did she have? Anna had to cut all ties. Had to chop that generational curse off at the roots and pray it stopped here, even if it meant she'd never have another baby, one she could keep. She forced her hand to stay away from the curve of her belly, because her uncle would notice. Notice and laugh, knowing she was weaker than her words.

"I have other things I need to do in town. I've said my piece. If you know what's good for you, you'll keep out of this." She marched through the door into the reception area.

"Or what? You'll sic a Delgado on me?" Uncle Paul chuckled. "I'm scared, Annie-girl. Absolutely terrified."

That did not deserve a reply.

Anna kept her head high as she stepped out onto the snowy sidewalk. She angled a speculating look at the clouded sky. Hopefully she'd have time to do her shopping, fit in coffee with Sabrina, and still get up the mountain before the next dump of snow began.

She laughed at herself. Look at her, reading the sky like a rancher after little more than a month of living close to nature.

"Anna Winter!" Dora Yanovich puffed out her name as she scurried closer.

Anna froze. This might be the last person who should see her exiting Paul's office.

"Are you thinking of buying property in town? And here I thought you were all snuggled in with that cowboy."

Anna stared at the meddling woman. "We're not living together." Why she needed to make that clear when her midsection bulged with Sawyer's child, she wasn't certain. Dora's assumptions didn't matter.

"I've got a perfect little rental I've been thinking of putting on the market. My Ivan, God rest his soul, left me with several properties, you know." Dora patted Anna's arm. "Not that I'm anywhere near as well off as those Delgados, but I do all right for myself, and the hair salon keeps me busy."

"Um, no... Thanks, though."

Dora leaned closer, thumbing toward Paul's office. "I know he's the only real estate agent in town, but you'd be better off with a private purchase. Paul Scarborough is not entirely scrupulous, if you get my meaning."

As though she needed this busybody to explain her family to her. "I'll keep that in mind. Excuse me. I really need to get going."

"You wouldn't believe the things I've heard. Why, just the other day, Krissy was complaining about his philandering ways while I colored her hair. Have you ever met her? That's Paul's wife, very reclusive. Still, I don't know how she puts up with him. Or him with her, come to think of it. She's such a mouse. But that's not what I was going to say. I was going to say that while I had her hair wrapped in foil, I couldn't help thinking of the last time I colored your hair. It's silly, I know, but for just a few seconds I thought this might be what you'd look like in twenty or thirty years. Minus all her rosacea and other blemishes. You do have beautiful skin, my dear, and I know you don't drink to excess as she does. I do hope you're remembering not to imbibe while pregnant. You don't want that baby to have fetal alcohol syndrome. Why—"

Anna managed to arrange her face in a hopefully neutral expression. "I'm not drinking. The baby is fine. Excuse me, Mrs. Yanovich, but I really must get back up River Road before the storm hits." She pivoted and strode away.

"But, Anna!"

Nope. She was not engaging in more conversation with that woman, no matter that she was Lauren's mother. It was a miracle Lauren turned out okay.

Anna pulled open the glass door of Manahan's Grocery and grabbed a shopping basket. She didn't dare glance over her shoulder for fear Dora had followed her. What if she'd said all that about Aunt Krissy in a busy place where other people could hear? Would those words stick in anyone's mind and cause them to speculate?

She couldn't take the chance. This would be her last trip to Saddle Springs before New Year's. Next time she'd drive right on through, all the way to Bozeman.

With Sawyer in the rearview mirror.

CHAPTER 19

Sawyer stared at his phone for several seconds. Adam Cavanagh. Ace had been the only reason they'd talked since leaving the rodeo circuit behind. Sawyer breathed a prayer and tapped to accept the call.

"Sawyer here."

"Dude. It's Adam."

"Yeah?"

"He's gone."

Sawyer leaned against the corral fence, his gaze blanking on the cows milling beyond. "No."

"Yeah. I was hoping he'd just sit up in that hospital bed and start talking, you know? Kept praying for that best possible outcome."

"You've been praying?"

"I have." Adam huffed a long breath into the phone. "This messed me up big time. I needed somewhere to turn."

"I get it. Me, too. Seems I somehow figured I was invincible before this. But if Ace wasn't... I couldn't be sure I was, either."

"I hear you. I'm flying to Texas for the funeral. Guess I need some closure."

"What day will it be? I should do that, too."

They made plans for a quick trip and ended the call.

Sawyer closed his eyes. The cold wind on his face reminded him he was alive. How could Ace not be? He and Adam and Ace had become close over the years on the circuit. Oh, the competition had been real. Each longed to win and had done everything he could to come out on top. Everything ethical, that is — nothing at the expense of the other guys.

How quickly situations changed. The memory of Ace's accident jabbed at Sawyer's mind. He'd been so busy at Eaglecrest — so busy trying to win his reluctant bride — that the potency had dimmed some, no longer sucking him in and spitting him out in cold sweat.

He welcomed the spiral now. It wasn't fair that Ace was dead and Sawyer was very much not. He bowed his head over the rail fence, feeling the weight on his shoulders. Watched the memory unfold. Remembered the swelling panic, the realization that no one could reach Ace in time. Hearing the bronc's hooves smash into his buddy. The pickup cowboys cutting the bronc away, too late, while the medics rushed the arena. The stretcher. The wail of the ambulance. The absolute silence for long moments while the audience sat in shock and the organizers made decisions. The fierce swell of apprehension as his name was called and he settled onto Excalibur, marked out, and signaled his readiness.

But he had not been ready. He'd never be ready again.

"Are you seeing something I'm not?" Kade's voice broke through the haze in Sawyer's mind. "That cow looks okay to me."

Cow? Sawyer blinked. Realized there was a cud-chewer staring warily back at him from ten feet away. "Uh... I wasn't looking at her."

His brother's shoulder bumped his. "Figured. What's up?"

"Ace passed on."

"Oh, man. No."

"Yeah. Adam just called. We're gonna fly down for the funeral." Sawyer shook his head. "I can't believe he's gone. There was never a man who loved life more than Ace Desjardins."

"I'm sorry."

Silence filled the air, broken only by the cows moving around in the snow-covered pasture. "Sometimes it's hard to hold onto hope."

His brother angled a look at him. "I get the feeling we're not talking rodeo anymore."

"Anna."

Kade nodded.

"How did you hold on through all that mess with Cheri?"

"Not very well at first, when she disappeared a week

before the wedding. She kicked my feet right out from under me."

"I remember." Sawyer had just graduated from Saddle Springs High. "I figured I'd never let a woman hold that much power over me."

Kade muffled a snort. "That worked out well for you."

"Didn't it, though?" Not really a question. Sawyer was all wrapped around Anna's little finger. He'd do anything for her. Anything to keep her and the baby in his life.

"What are you going to do?"

"Ain't that the question? Maybe a few days away will give me perspective. I'll take some time to really pray for peace. Here in the thick of things, I just bounce around. I want God's best. I really do. But when I'm near Anna and see her body swollen with my child — well, I'm not proud of it, but the fact remains. I want that more."

His brother nodded. "I'm really sorry Cheri and I messed things up a couple of weeks ago. I mean, it was a genuine offer — still is — but you had asked me to drop it. I didn't communicate that clearly with my wife."

"She has a mind of her own."

"She does. But she means well."

Sawyer glanced over at Kade. "Do you want to know why I hate you sometimes?"

"Hate me? That's rather strong."

"You're so nice. So forgiving. I've tried to believe that was a sign of weakness, but I'm finally starting to realize it isn't. Not really. I made sure to be anything but nice. And, yeah, not so forgiving, either. You forgave Cheri. I don't think I'd have been a big enough man to do that."

"It didn't come easy, bro. I was so blindsided. So broken, and it was all her fault."

Sawyer nodded, remembering.

"I was pretty sure I'd never be happy again. And, if by any chance happiness came my way, I wouldn't be able to trust it. So with Daniela..."

"You were just doing a good deed."

"Mostly. I desperately wanted a family, but I couldn't fall in love and be vulnerable."

"So you married a dying pregnant woman."

"Sounds like I took advantage of the situation." Kade shrugged slightly. "It was my chance to make a grand gesture and get a baby out of the deal. I didn't expect to fall in love with Daniela. I mean, I knew she was dying when we first met."

"You already knew you were going to be hurt."

"Yeah. And I figured I deserved pain. You know? But I was willing to care for her and take her baby as my own, and I grew to love her. Also, have you seen Jericho lately? I don't resent choosing him for one red hot second. That kid is mine."

"He's awesome. He really is. The thing is, Anna's baby is mine. He's got Delgado blood. Every time God asks me to submit to His will, I just can't let go completely. How could it possibly not be His will for us to be a family? For my child not to know me as his father?"

"I can't answer that, bro. That kind of full trust... I don't know where it comes from. It's not just one decision. It's a day-in, day-out attitude of knowing God is our Father and He loves us far more than we could ever love our own kids. He's not cackling in glee as He punishes us. Not until we surrender do we begin to see the bigger picture."

"What kind of bigger picture are we talking here? This is a living human being. How much more important can it be"

Kade looked down, shaking his head. "If I knew, I'd tell you."

"Ace didn't even have a chance to grapple with any decisions before the accident. Vanessa was such a—" He cut off the word. "I hope she can live with herself and what she did to Ace. She got pregnant on purpose to drag him down and extort money out of him. Now that he's gone, she's playing the grieving common-law wife while she petitions for Ace's child to be declared his heir."

"What she did to him was despicable."

"And the timing. Why did she choose right before the most important ride of his career to drop that gem on him? It's like she was *trying* to get him killed."

"You've got to let it go, bro. Pray for her. Pray for her to meet Jesus. Pray for that innocent child."

Sawyer shook his head. "I don't know if I can do that. Vanessa trapped him. She did it willfully. And it seems like she's getting away with murder. How can I forgive her?"

ANNA EDGED FURTHER AWAY from the barn's Dutch doors, flung open at the top to let in fresh air. She'd come out to check the barn records, since one of the reports hadn't synced with the office computer. She hadn't meant to eavesdrop. Not really... but she'd paused when she heard her name. Melted a little inside at the raw anguish in Sawyer's voice as he told his brother about fighting with God.

She knew what that felt like. She'd been fighting, too, and she'd finally come to the conclusion — again — that she had to come clean, no matter what. Throw herself on God's mercy. Sawyer's mercy. His family's mercy.

But.

Vanessa trapped him. She did it willfully. How can I forgive her?

She backed up another step. She'd been fooling herself — Sawyer wouldn't show mercy. How could she bear to see his lips tighten? His voice harden? It would be much, much easier to escape while he was away in Texas, even if that meant she had to raise this child alone.

Another step back, and her boots knocked a metal bucket against the barn's stone foundation. It rattled as it tipped and rolled.

Anna froze, staring at the light-filled rectangle. Maybe the cows crunching through the snow while munching on hay had muffled the clank.

"What was that?"

Her lack of luck held. She grabbed the knob on the barn office door, twisted, and pushed. It flew back against the wall, another much-too-loud sound. She darted inside, shut the door, and leaned against it, her chest heaving at the sudden spurt of action.

The baby let its shock and discomfort be known with a sharp kick to her ribs.

There was no getting around what she'd done.

The knob rattled as the door pushed against her. "Who's in here?" Sawyer's voice. "Everything okay?"

Would he leave if she ignored him? Not likely, when she blocked the door. She was terrible at subterfuge. "Fine. Don't worry about a thing." Like that wasn't a giveaway. She might as well have added that she hadn't been listening to a word they said.

"Anna?" His voice softened. "What's up?"

"Nothing." She sidled away from the door. "Just came out to check why the records aren't syncing. Has there been a problem with the ranch network that you know of?"

He swung the door open, his dark eyes assessing her, piercing into her soul. Then he glanced at the older computer sitting on the workbench. "It's not even turned on."

"I just got out here."

Sawyer's eyebrows punched up behind the brim of his cowboy hat.

Keep him distracted. "It's set to sync as it shuts down. Right?"

"Yeah, I think so. Maybe there's too much snow on the satellite dish."

"That could be." She heaved a mental sigh of relief. "Would you mind clearing it if that's what happened? I'll get the machine booted up."

"No problem." He studied her a few seconds longer before leaving the small office, pulling the door behind him.

Anna dropped onto the backless stool and lowered her head against her arms on the desk. What was she—

"Sweetheart?"

She surged upright and turned to see Sawyer leaning in the doorway. The baby prodded her again. "Oh, you scared me."

He eyed her. "You seem mighty jumpy today."

"Me? Not really." She scrambled for an excuse that would make sense to him and get her off the hook. "The baby... it's super active today. It keeps jabbing me. Hard."

Sawyer's gaze softened as it dropped to her hands caressing her belly. His voice turned wistful. "Can I feel?"

"Um, sure. You can try. It's a lot stronger than last week." She unzipped her parka and waited for him to strip off his gloves. Then she placed his hand just below her ribs. There. The baby punched out a solid kick. Sawyer ought to feel that.

A look of wonder crossed his face. "Wow." He closed his eyes and absorbed more of the action. "I can't believe it."

Why couldn't she just go with this? He'd be an awesome daddy. Look how much Kade and Cheri's kids adored him.

Vanessa trapped him. She did it willfully. How can I forgive her?

Oh, yeah. That. Anna backed up, ramming her hip into the desk, breaking the contact.

Sawyer's eyes flew open, his face still the softest she'd ever seen. He cradled her cheeks between his palms and stepped back into her space. "Anna, our baby..."

"I-I know."

His lips brushed hers, but she turned her head away.

His kisses trailed across her cheek. "I can't let that little tyke go, sweetheart. I can't let *you* go."

Anna set her hands on his chest and gave a little push. "Don't."

"It's so right. *We're* so right. Give me a chance to prove it to you."

How can I forgive her?

"I need to check the computer."

His breath warmed her cheek as he brushed his lips just below her ear. "It can wait."

"Sawyer, stop."

He stilled for a second then pulled back enough to look at her. "What can possibly be more important than giving *our son* a stable home with two parents who love him?" Sawyer's voice hardened with every word, his eyes matching the transformation.

Anna shuddered and looked away.

Sawyer lifted her chin, not quite as gently as he had in the past. "You're driving me crazy, woman."

Sorry? But best to keep silent.

"You're not just playing hard to get, are you? There's more going on. I'll get to the bottom of it, Anna Winter. Because I'm not going to let you throw away my chance for a relationship with my son. You don't want him? Fine. He's mine. I'll raise him myself."

She scrunched her eyes shut and shook her head, a quick, jerky movement.

"And why not?" Ice filled his voice. "You're denying me what I want the most. I have rights, too, you know. It's not all about you. You are only one of the three people affected by what's happening, and that's not even counting my family. Denying my parents their grandchild. Denying

Kade and Trevor their nephew. I won't let you do it, Anna. I won't."

"You promised."

"Yeah?" His tone solidified like cooling molten rock. "Well, I changed my mind."

CHAPTER 20

D o you miss this?" Sawyer sat on the top tier of the stands overlooking the Texas arena, elbows on his knees. The place was empty except for an attendant picking up trash.

"Not as much as I thought I would." Adam shook his head. "Which is weird, since I couldn't imagine a different life until that night."

"Same. I mean, I knew rodeo's a young guy's sport, and my time was coming."

"It wasn't the slower reflexes of old age that got Desjardins."

"I know." Sawyer huffed a sigh. "Did you see her? Dressed all in black, and that ghastly makeup job totally designed to make her look pathetic."

"Don't forget the lace hanky to dab her eyes. You think Ace's mom bought into the whole performance?"

"That's what kills me the most. She looked so bereft. But Vanessa managed to prove that she'd been living in

Ace's apartment for over a year, that they were officially shacked up even though his mother didn't know it."

"She lied."

"We know that, but the judge believed her. If I'd known there was a hearing, I'd have come down and testified."

"Yeah, she hid what she was doing. Ready for Hollywood, that one. Good at what she does." Adam's grunt doubled as a snarl. "Makes me so mad."

"At least she's not faking pregnancy, right? And they ran the DNA and proved the baby is Ace's."

"Is that kind of test accurate, you think?"

"Yeah. I looked it up." Sawyer took off his hat and twisted it in his hands. "Been thinking of having Anna tested, though she swears the baby is mine."

Adam raised his eyebrows. "You don't believe her?"

"I don't know. She just doesn't make any sense. We've got the chemistry. I can't figure out why she refuses to marry me."

His friend chuckled. "Sorry. I know it's not funny, but I'm engaged and it's all fake. Where you'd give anything to be in my boots. Except, you know, real."

"Fake? What are you talking about?"

"Aw, Riley and I are just helping each other out. Being engaged is giving me some leverage with my old man, and it's giving her time to figure out some stuff, too. Once my stepdad signs my dad's ranch over to me and my brothers, we'll break up, and she'll leave. It'll all work out."

"So you're going around kissing a girl you have no intention of marrying?"

"Yup." Adam flashed him a grin, his eyebrows bobbing. "And she really gets into it."

"Sounds like a recipe for a disaster, if you ask me."

"Nobody did. At least we're honest with each other. We both know it's temporary. We agreed right from the start, so neither of us will be blindsided when the day comes to have our big fight and break up."

"She seriously means nothing to you?"

"I wouldn't go quite that far. She's a lot of fun. Spunky, and she can stick to a horse like nobody's business." Adam elbowed Sawyer. "You went and picked a girl who can't ride. Some kind of wrangler you are."

"Even in June, I guess I knew there was more to life than the circuit."

"Yeah, whatever made Sawyer Delgado feel good."

Hard to deny. "You're one to talk. You went through a girlfriend a month until that mess with the Nashville singer."

"Chantelle Devereaux? She was sure something. Curves like Dolly Parton."

"Brains like... well, never mind. I could name half a dozen popular singers, but I don't want to slander anyone. Chantelle definitely isn't the brightest thing with a double X."

"Word. Riley's definitely a big step up. She's real."

"Or fake."

"Both, I guess." Adam turned and looked at him. "What are you going to do about Anna?"

"Man, I wish I knew. I might've let my frustration show

the other day. Told her I'd raise the baby myself. She could be part of it or not, her choice."

Adam's eyes bugged out. "You'd take on a newborn? There's no way I'd do that."

"My brother did and survived. Not saying it will be easy, but I can't just sign away my own son."

"Tough spot."

"You're telling me. Don't get Riley pregnant, dude. It complicates everything beyond belief."

"We're not sleeping together. As far as I know, I haven't left a woman prego. And after Ace... well, I'm smarter than I once was. Turned over a new leaf. Talking to God and all."

"Me, too, but my smarts came a little too late." Sawyer stared down at the silent arena with the holding pens beyond, seeing it alive with action, hearing the announcer and the crowd, smelling the sweat, the horses, the leather. Tasting the adrenaline rush.

He could live without the hype and buzz. Becoming a father was all that and more. Single parenting would be the wildest ride he'd ever been on, and it would last eighteen years, not eight seconds. He'd get bucked off a time or two, no doubt, but he'd hit the dirt rolling and swing right back into the saddle.

Would he rather do it with Anna? Yeah, for sure. And he wasn't done trying to convince her to team up for life. But if he had to raise his son solo, then he would.

"My stepbrother only sees his kid on weekends."

Sawyer blinked Adam back into focus. "Oh?"

"His ex drops Toby off at the ranch Friday afternoons, and Travis returns him to town Sunday afternoons."

"That's rough."

"Yeah, Travis wasn't really into it at first, what with the diapers and all." Adam cocked his eyebrows at Sawyer. "Or so I hear. I wasn't around much. But now, the kid is three. He kind of lights up the place when he's there."

"Your brother is okay with all that? Does he still love the boy's mother?"

"Me an' Trav don't talk much. No love lost between us, and definitely no heart-to-heart going on. He's my step-dad's oldest, and he hated like stink when his dad married my mom, 'cause I'm older than him. Not that Declan looks at me as his firstborn, I can tell you that."

"I remember you telling me about your stepdad. Sounds like a real winner."

Adam shook his head. "You've never met a man more driven. He works as hard as he expects all of us to. My mom — well, that's another story. If it wasn't for my twin sisters, I don't know if she'd stick it out."

"Is she doing any better with you home? I know she hated you being away all the time."

"Honestly? I've been shocked at how withdrawn she is, even with the twins. They're thirteen and running wild." Adam drove his hands through his hair. "She doesn't even seem to notice. Declan toed the line hard and fast with us boys, but the girls just laugh in his face. He has no clue how to handle them except bluster and threaten some more, and that doesn't work. My mother ignores it all."

Sawyer couldn't imagine his mom fading into an inactive, ineffectual part of Eaglecrest. But, then, he also couldn't imagine his dad forcing his will upon his wife or boys. He looked over at Adam. "What're you going to do?"

"I need to get Declan to sign my dad's ranch over to the twins and me. He rented out the home place but he runs all the land. When I can take possession, I'll bring my mother home with me."

"You'd split up their marriage?"

Adam rolled his eyes. "Dude, that's been over for ten years. She should never have married him to begin with, but she thought she was doing what was best for us boys when our dad died and left her with a load of debt. She wouldn't listen to me. I was just a snot-nosed kid who obviously needed a father. Even at thirteen, I knew Declan Cavanagh was nothing but trouble."

"And yet you took his name."

"Didn't want to. I've thought a few times about taking my birth name back to honor my dad, but I've gone by Cavanagh so long now it seems pointless. It's just a name."

"Dude, I don't know what to say. I hope your thing with Riley works out so you get your dad's ranch back. So long as you remember you're playing with fire."

"Don't I know it." Adam huffed a long sigh and jabbed Sawyer with his elbow. "Hope your thing with Anna works out, too. I'll get to praying for you both."

"Thanks, and backatcha. We're only two weeks out from the end of the year. Time's running out."

"I'll pray, man. And for the baby. You said the ultrasound showed it was a boy?"

Sawyer shook his head. "Anna refused to find out."

Adam let out a guffaw. "So you're guessing. Dude, you are gonna be some surprised when it comes out a girl."

"Not gonna happen."

I'LL BE HOME on Friday. We need to talk.

Anna stared at Sawyer's text. They did *not* need to talk. They'd been talking for eight weeks and he was just as stubborn now as he'd been at the beginning. She'd thought it was a matter of outlasting him... until his final shot before leaving for Texas.

You don't want him? Fine. He's mine. I'll raise him myself.

She hadn't seen that coming, never in a million years. Not even knowing his brother Kade had raised a newborn. She didn't need to agree, but what kind of jerk did that make her? They'd had a deal. They both had to agree to any new plan or he'd sign the papers still tucked in the top drawer of her dresser.

I've changed my mind.

So he'd changed the rules. He had no intention of signing, no matter what. Period, full stop. Didn't that make any agreement on her side null and void, too?

She paced the apartment from one end to the other. The windows on the north overlooked the parking area between the garage, house, and stables. Snow sifted gently down, caught in the glow of the yard lights illuminating the area. She pivoted away.

Her choice — adoption — was not a possibility without his acquiescence. His first choice — marriage — sounded lovely until she thought about decades of keeping her secret. She couldn't do it. Which left her — or him — raising the child alone.

Could she really walk away in March and leave the baby with Sawyer? Her heart cried out. She couldn't. Placing the baby with strangers was hard enough to contemplate, but giving it up to the man she loved?

She did love him. She might have used him in June to get what she thought would be a relatively easy out of her predicament but, in the past couple of months, she'd seen the real Sawyer. The tenderhearted rock with unflinching focus on building a family with her and their baby.

It would be cruel to keep the child separated from its father. And Sawyer would never stand for it. He'd move in next door if he had to, even if that meant leaving the ranch he loved. He wouldn't leave his child without a father. If Anna's life remained that entwined with Sawyer's, she might as well marry him.

Could she trust him with her secret?

Oh, how she wished she could, but the harshness in his voice as he spoke of Vanessa suggested otherwise. He'd been harsh with Anna, too, in the aftermath, when he'd pulled their agreement out from beneath her.

The only way to get Sawyer out of her life — without the adoption — was to give him full custody. Then she could be the absentee parent and escape to live her own life, free from all responsibility.

But that wasn't right. She deserved to suffer. She was the one who carried the mantle of the generational curse, not him.

Anna turned to the awkward little tree, only made beautiful by Sawyer's treasures and his care in decorating it for her. She fingered the nearest horseshoe frame, where a little boy in a red cowboy hat grinned out with a winsome face.

None of this was the baby's fault. Didn't their child deserve a happy, carefree childhood like his father'd had? Sawyer could give the baby that, right here at Eaglecrest with a doting extended family.

Anna could give the baby a thieving alcoholic for a grandmother. Why did the curse have to be so real?

Another ornament caught her eye, a star cut from wood and decorated with glitter paint. A childish hand had written on it with a black marker, the words squishing down into one corner. *Wise men still seek Him.*

She stared at the star, remembering the story of the wise men following it to the child Jesus. They'd traveled a long way, bringing gifts, pursuing a chance to worship Him in person.

Had she ever pursued worship with that kind of dedication? Not really. The initial joy she'd felt back in September had quickly been displaced by regret and fear. Instead of checking in with her godly mentor, she'd come to her own conclusions, latching onto the only course of action that could come close to atoning for what she'd done. Had that been wisdom or more of a whim?

Anna sank to the ottoman beside the tree. There was the beaded candle, reminding her that Jesus was the light of the world. An angel crafted of wire and twine, a token of the heavenly host so gloriously announcing the Savior's birth. The evergreen tree itself promised a hope that would never die.

Hadn't the pastor said Jesus died for everyone? That His sacrifice covered all sins? Surely, she wasn't the most messed-up person in the world. Was there hope? How could she find out?

CHAPTER 21

Anna inched down the winding mountain road amid snow angling across the beams from her headlights. These were definitely not the best driving conditions, but if she waited, Sawyer would arrive back at Eaglecrest.

She'd thought through every single believer she knew in Saddle Springs. Denae and Cheri were too close to the situation. Lauren Carmichael was Dora's daughter. She wasn't a blabbermouth like her mother, but she did tend to prying and bluntness. Tori Morrison sat at her dying mother-in-law's bedside. Anna wasn't that close to Carmen Haviland, plus the Rocking H was across the valley and up another steep mountain road. What if Carmen couldn't help?

That left knocking on the church office door and talking to Pastor Roland or his wife. They were nice enough, but they were close friends of the Delgados. She couldn't put them in such an awkward spot.

No, she'd return to Bozeman, to the church where she'd

knelt at the altar all those months ago. The church she should have kept attending rather than assuming she could take it on her own from here.

She'd packed up her clothes, since she didn't know how long it would take, but she'd left the papers on top of the dresser. They were no good to her without Sawyer's scrawl on the bottom. And maybe she didn't want it there, anyway. Her thoughts ricocheted like a ball in a pinball machine. Maybe this... no, that... or possibly the other thing.

How could she really know what was right?

By contrast, Saddle Springs lay still in the sifting snow as she drove through, for all the world like a postcard. The highway had been plowed, so she breathed a prayer of thanks and picked up a little speed. Bozeman lay a solid four hours away under good conditions. These were not good conditions.

SAWYER THUMBED his phone off airplane mode as they taxied to the gate. Message after message popped up on his display. Whoa. What had been going on at Eaglecrest in the hours he'd been in the air?

Mom: *Where is Anna?*

Denae: *Did you and Anna have a fight?*

Kade: *Dude. I hope you've heard from Anna.*

The icy runway had nothing on the chill clenching Sawyer's heart. He tapped his mother's number.

"You've landed?" was all the greeting she gave him.

"Yes. We haven't started deplaning yet. What's going on?"

"I hoped you'd know."

Sawyer rubbed his jaw. "She's missing?" How could that be?

From the window seat, Adam's eyebrows shot up as he focused on Sawyer.

"She's taken all her stuff. She didn't leave a note, just the adoption papers on the dresser."

His gut twisted. "You went inside?"

"She didn't come over for breakfast. Then I noticed her car wasn't in its usual spot. It had been gone long enough there weren't even any tracks visible in the snow. I texted her then phoned, and she didn't answer either one. So, yes, I went into the apartment when she didn't open the door, either."

"But she can't have left. We have an agreement." One he'd already informed her he was breaking. He sagged back into the airplane seat and closed his eyes as dread swamped him. Had his stubbornness pushed her over the edge?

Adam nudged him. "Our turn to deplane."

"Mom, I've got to go. I'll try and get ahold of her and get back to you. Pray."

"We have been and will keep at it." Her voice held deep concern. "Love you, son."

"Thanks." Sawyer stood, shoved his phone in his pocket, and pulled his carry-on out of the open overhead bin.

Adam edged out behind him. "What's going on?"

"Anna left the ranch with all her stuff and didn't tell anyone. And she's not picking up calls."

"Dude. That's bad."

"You're telling me." Sawyer exited the aircraft, barely remembering to nod his thanks to the attendants. Once in the jetway, he pulled out his case's telescoping handle and fell in step beside his friend. "She must've gone back to Bozeman, but why?"

"Bozeman?"

"Yeah, she left her apartment there set up. She's kept up her rent." He'd made sure she had more than enough pay to cover it. "I just don't know if I should follow her there or leave her be."

"Do you love her?"

Sawyer shot his friend a hard glare. "Now we're talking mush and feelings?"

"Yo. We're talking reality. Declan may not believe it, but even guys have emotions. I've experienced one or two myself."

They made their way toward the terminal doors. Sawyer paused inside as snow gusted past the glass. "I sure hate to think of anyone driving in this."

"Might be better to figure out where she is for sure. Maybe she has friends in Spokane and headed that way."

"She's never mentioned any, and the passes west into Idaho will be even uglier than I-90 eastbound."

"If she's trying to hide, Bozeman is the one place she *won't* be. You can't go chasing her around the Pacific Northwest without a clue where she's gone. Ever heard of looking for a needle in a haystack?"

Sawyer growled his frustration. Of course, she'd be headed east. That was the only logical direction. But a woman who ran away on a snowy day wasn't ruled by logic. He hated when he might be wrong. He hated the feeling of helplessness. He hated being rejected.

Eaglecrest was the opposite direction. He'd save the hour's drive twice over if he just headed east now.

And what was he going to do when he caught up with her? If he even did? Kiss her. Beg her. Threaten her. None of those things had worked for the past eight weeks. Why would today be any different? He'd tried so hard to understand, but she refused to give him anything solid to go on.

Sawyer pulled his jacket out of his pack and shrugged it on. Sure hadn't needed the thing in Texas. He pulled out his phone to move it to the jacket pocket and stared at it. Would she pick up for him? Doubtful, but he had to try. He tapped her number and listened to it ring. Once. Twice. Three times. Voicemail.

"Hey, sweetheart." He tried to keep his tone breezy, like he didn't even know she'd bolted. "Just landed in Missoula, and I can't wait to see you again soon." That was the unvarnished truth. "Give me a call."

Adam rolled his eyes as he zipped up his parka. "You are such an optimist."

"You know what? I can't just let her go. That would be all kinds of wrong."

"Well, you can't go chasing her without a plan, either. Because that's all kinds of stupid."

"You might be right. So, I'm hoping God's got some plans, because I'm plum out."

"Headed up to Eaglecrest then?"

Sawyer grimaced. "Yeah. Gonna get a prayer meeting on in the meanwhile."

"Keep in touch. And if you're talking to God anyway, say a prayer Declan will see the light soon and give me my due so Riley can go on her way."

"You really want her to leave?"

Adam shook his head. "Doesn't matter what I want. A deal's a deal, and she's only sticking around for what she'll get out of it. She's just putting on a performance for my old man."

"You sure?"

"Yeah." Adam closed the space to the doors, which slid open at his approach.

Sawyer followed him out into blowing snow. Welcome home to Montana, where the weather matched his heart.

Sawyer took the exit off the highway into Saddle Springs then turned down a street that offered a shortcut to the fairgrounds by the bridge. He drove past Shear Inspirations, where Sabrina shoveled the sidewalk.

He hadn't even thought of Anna's friend this whole hour. Anna hadn't mentioned her very often in the past couple of months. Maybe they'd seen each other when Anna came to town, though. In fact, maybe Anna was holed up at Sabrina's place right now. He swerved the truck into the unplowed snow at the edge of the street and clambered out.

Sabrina leaned on the long handle. "Hey, Sawyer."

"Hi. Let me give you a hand." He reached for the shovel, and she let him have it. He made two passes before glancing over to where she stood, arms wrapped around herself. "Seen Anna lately?"

Her gaze turned wary. "Not for a while, no. Why?"

Maybe they weren't that close. Maybe Anna hadn't confided in Sabrina. In that case, he shouldn't be the one to air their laundry.

"Just wondered. I've been out of town for a few days and haven't heard from her much." Like at all.

The salon door pushed open, wafting warm air onto the sidewalk along with the jingling of bells. "Saw-yer!" Dora Yanovich sing-songed.

He forced a smile to his lips. "Hi, Mrs. Yanovich."

"Thank you for helping Sabrina out. You're such a good boy. I was just telling Anna that the other day. I could hardly believe she was looking for property to buy when she had you all wrapped up!"

Sawyer stared at the older woman. Of all the things he expected to hear, this was so not one of them. "Come again?"

The smirk she offered was that of a cat preparing to pounce on a mouse. "She was coming out of the real estate office when I saw her. What other reason would she have for being in there? Although when I offered her a deal on my little house over on Pine Street, she didn't seem interested."

Anything you say in front of this woman can be used against you.

"That's interesting." Sawyer scooped the last load of

snow off the edge of the sidewalk and handed the shovel back to Sabrina. "I hope you ladies have a great afternoon, what's left of it."

"Thanks for the help."

If there was any message in Sabrina's expression, he couldn't read it. He tipped his hat and beelined back for the truck as the two women retreated into the salon. Now what?

Well, first, he shouldn't do his thinking where Dora could watch and speculate, so he started the truck and drove around the corner. The only real estate business in town belonged to Paul Scarborough. Dillon's father. And Dillon had come out of the doctor's office with Anna a month ago, acting like he knew Anna well and had a right to be there. Anna's answers to Sawyer's questions had been vague, but he'd thought she'd been telling the truth that there was nothing between her and Dillon.

Now? Now he wasn't so sure, because something was not adding up.

Two blocks down, he parked in front of the realty office. Right next to the medical clinic. Huh.

Maybe he should drive up to Eaglecrest and think this through. Pray about it before saying something he might regret. On the other hand, he was here right now. The office lights were on, so Paul was likely in.

Sawyer strode into the office, past the receptionist's vacant station, and stopped in the open doorway beyond with his arms across his chest.

Paul Scarborough's feet came off his desk and landed on the floor with a thump as the man's shock turned to an amused grin. "Well, well. If it isn't the young buck Sawyer Delgado."

He nodded. "Mr. Scarborough."

"What can I do for you? Looking for some property?"

Sawyer skewered the man with a narrowed glare. "My guess is you know exactly why I'm here."

"Oh?" The man raised his eyebrows. "And what's that?"

"Tell me about your son's relationship to Anna."

Paul tilted his chair back and laughed. "It goes back quite a ways."

The guy was enjoying this far too much. Maybe he needed help wiping that smirk off his face. Maybe he needed to realize the joke was up.

Sawyer's fists clenched as he took a step closer. Only then did he realize Paul was not alone in his office. A woman with unkempt graying hair stared up at him in bewilderment.

"I'm guessing you two haven't met." Paul motioned between the woman and Sawyer.

She had a somewhat familiar look to her, but Sawyer couldn't place it. Paul's wife? If so, she'd changed quite a bit. For one thing, Krissy Scarborough was portly, and this woman was thin as a rail. She rose unsteadily to her feet, balancing herself with a hand on the edge of the desk. "Sawyer Delgado? I've heard about you."

"You have the advantage of me."

She spat on his boots.

What on earth? Why did Paul have this crazy woman in his office? Was she one of the women he was rumored to be sleeping with? Why would he pick someone who didn't even take care of herself? Someone who looked a lot like his wife, though Sawyer hadn't met his wife very many times. To call her reclusive was kind.

Paul chuckled. "Let me make the official introductions. Sawyer, I'd like you to meet my wife's sister, Penny Winter."

Penny *Winter?* Click. Click, click.

Sawyer realized his mouth was hanging open, and he snapped it shut. He should say something, but nothing coherent came to mind. He pivoted and marched out of the office, stopping along the sidewalk to slide his boot through a bank of soft snow to scuff off the saliva.

He climbed into his truck and pulled away from the curb, his brain swirling with so many implications. What on earth should he do with this information?

Besides pray. Really pray. That was a given.

CHAPTER 22

Anna curled on her bed in her Bozeman apartment. She'd hauled a couple of boxes up the three flights of stairs. The rest would have to wait. She was exhausted.

This space had never felt less like home. A few days before Christmas, and there wasn't a single strand of lights, not one ornament, and definitely not a lopsided, whimsically decorated tree.

Oh, Sawyer. She'd been over halfway home — wasn't that a misnomer? — when his call had come in. His voicemail had come through on her Bluetooth. *Hey, sweetheart...*

Her heart clenched. He'd have to wait a little longer. Possibly it was too late. But she had to figure herself out before she could beg his forgiveness. No. That was the stinkin' thinkin' that had spiraled her into this mess. She needed a new perspective. She had to figure *God* out first.

There was no time to lose. She reached for her phone, trying not to see all the texts and calls from Sawyer's family as she searched her contact list. There she was. Olive Mueller.

Anna breathed a desperate prayer and tapped the number. It rang twice before the older woman's voice came on.

"Is that really you, Anna? Praise the Lord."

"It's me." A tear slithered down her cheek. "Do you have time to get together? I... I need help. Good counsel."

"For you, always time. You are back in town?"

"Yes." Anna dabbed her eyes. "I'm sorry that I didn't answer your calls. How I assumed I knew best. I'm sorry for everything."

"Oh, my girl. You are forgiven. May I come over and bring supper to share? Perhaps in an hour or so?"

She didn't deserve a friend like Olive, but maybe life wasn't all about merit, after all. "Please. I'd like that."

"See you soon."

Anna hauled two more boxes up from the car, took a shower, and ran a duster over the living room surfaces before hearing Olive's knock. She opened the door and found herself enveloped in a fierce hug by the tall, thin woman.

Olive leaned back and looked at Anna. "You look good. Tired, but good. And my, how the little one has grown! Have you been taking care of the both of you?"

Not really, but Sawyer had done his best.

Anna blinked away the ever-present tears. "I'm trying, but I need help." Had she ever in her life uttered those words before?

Her friend nodded then bent to pick up a pair of paper

bags at her feet. "I seem to remember a fondness for Greek food, so I have brought souvlaki and rice pilaf and salad. I hope the baby likes tzatziki!"

Anna's mouth watered from the delicious aromas as Olive set the bags on the kitchen counter. "I'm sure it does."

Olive turned, her thin eyebrows high. "It? Your baby is not an it, my girl. You may not know whether you are having a boy or a girl, but definitely not an it."

Honesty began right here. "I've been trying to keep my distance. Emotionally."

Olive began plating the food. "How is that working for you?"

"Not very well." Anna sniffled. "Especially since it — he or she — has become so active. It's a real person. Inside me."

"Created by God for a purpose."

"I have a hard time with that. Because I feel it was created by me in a fit of desperation and lust. God had very little to do with the situation."

Olive's finger wove back and forth as she shook her head. "God may not have caused it, but He wants to be glorified in your life through what has happened. He wants to use the situation to draw you close to Him. He loves you with an everlasting love. Here." She thrust a plate at Anna. "Let's have a seat, and I'll pray for our talk."

It was going to be one of those evenings where tears were going to gush. Anna should be getting used to water-works by now, since her hormones had been such a mess throughout her pregnancy. But, for the first time in months, she felt the tears might be cathartic.

She would tell Olive everything and throw herself on the woman's mercy and, by extension, God's.

It took a while for his brothers to show up. He supposed that was reasonable. Kade had little kids to tuck in bed, and Trevor had been exercising the second last mount of the day when Sawyer called. He'd picked up the slack when Sawyer had left for Texas.

Now, Trevor grabbed a decaf off the kitchen island and turned to Sawyer. "What's going on?"

Kade, already sitting at the table, nodded.

Mom twisted her hands together.

Sawyer turned to his dad. "Could you please pray?"

"Absolutely." His father, seated at the head of the table, closed his eyes. "Our loving heavenly Father, You've said that where two or three are gathered in Your name, You're present in the midst of us. We welcome You here and ask for Your wisdom. Lord, whatever happens in this situation with Sawyer and Anna and their baby, we pray that You will be glorified. In Jesus' name, amen."

"Amen," whispered Mom.

When Sawyer didn't speak up immediately, Kade jumped in. "Have you talked to Anna? Where is she?"

"I left a message on her voicemail, and I've texted a few times."

Kade's shoulder slumped. "So you don't know where she is."

"No. I mean, my best guess is that she's in Bozeman, but I'm not actually certain. Adam pointed out that without knowing for sure, I could be on a wild goose chase over nasty winter roads." He took a deep breath. "And, besides, I've done all the chasing and pushing and ordering, and look where that's gotten me."

Silence for a moment, broken by Mom's quiet voice. "That's what she ran from."

How admitting that killed him. "Seems so."

"So... this little gathering here." Trevor circled the table with his finger. "Is to tell us you don't know anything? Dude, a text would have sufficed."

Dad shot a warning glare at his oldest son.

Sawyer shook his head. "There's more. Ever since October, I've been baffled why she wouldn't marry me." He narrowed his gaze at his brothers. "You can laugh all you want, but what we've got is more than an unexpected pregnancy. We've got chemistry, and I know she's not immune to it. And she's mentioned a few things about coming to faith recently, so we've got that in common, too. So, what was holding her back from saying yes?"

Trevor and Kade looked at each other and shrugged. "I've wondered the same," Trevor offered. "I mean, who knows what she saw in you to begin with, but she obviously found something. Why wouldn't she take that all the way to the bank?"

Interesting choice of words.

Kade folded his hands on the table and leaned forward. "What Cheri and I have never been able to figure out is how Dillon Scarborough fits in. I am so not calling you a liar for saying you saw them together, bro, but that piece just doesn't add up. Cheri was all set to ask Dillon, but I talked her out of it. Harmony didn't need to hear that kind of conversation."

"Bingo." Sawyer pointed his finger at Kade. "Dillon is significant. You know why?"

His family exchanged looks and shook their heads.

"Because Dillon's mother and Anna's mother are sisters."

"*What?*"

"No way. You're kidding."

"How on earth...?"

He held up both hands. "Hear me out. I prayed all the way home from the airport. Prayed for Anna's safety. Prayed for comfort and wisdom. Man, I had over an hour. I prayed for everything I could think of in between worrying the bits of intel I had like a dog with a bone. I came into town and saw Sabrina shoveling the walk in front of the salon. *Hey*, I thought. *Maybe she knows something.* So I pulled over and finished up the snow removal."

"And...?" prompted Kade.

"Dora Yanovich came out. That woman is such a gossip and she loves nothing more than stirring up trouble." Sawyer caught his mother's raised eyebrows. "Mom, you know it's true. She could hardly wait to tell me Anna was thinking of buying property in town and wondered if I thought it was strange."

"*I* think it's strange, and I don't know Anna that well."

Trevor rolled his eyes. "Why would you believe Dora?"

"Most gossip has a root in something real, however small the kernel. Dora said she'd seen Anna coming out of the real estate office. And since her comment reminded me that Paul is Dillon's father, I pulled around the block and thought I'd ask a few questions."

"And?" prompted Kade, his gaze narrowed.

"I asked him how his son knew Anna, and he found that quite humorous. I was ready to punch him out and wipe that smirk off his face." Glancing at his mother, Sawyer held up both hands. "I wouldn't have. Just saying I was tempted."

"Bro, I understand the appeal," said Kade. "Like father, like son."

"Turned out there was someone else in the office I hadn't seen at first. Paul took great pleasure in introducing me to his wife's sister, Penny Winter." He waited a heartbeat for it to sink in. "Anna's mother."

"For real?" Kade sat back.

"Yeah. For real."

"So what did she say?" Trevor wanted to know. "Kick you in the butt for ruining her daughter? Hug you for being the great guy that you are?"

"She spat on my boots."

"No way."

"Yes way. Here's the thing. If I don't miss my guess, she's a druggie. At the very least, she's a solid mess. At the worst... who knows?"

Kade looked thoughtful. "Is there any sign that Anna's on drugs, or has been?"

"I'd say no." Sawyer turned to his mom. "You've been working with her. Any clues I might have missed?"

"I really don't think so. My only concern has been that she sneaks a lot of junk food, especially ice cream."

"A weakness for tutti-frutti isn't the same as an addiction to cocaine."

Mom laughed. "I'm aware. Just saying that nothing I noticed pointed to anything serious."

"Here's the thing," Trevor said. "Was she hiding her relatives from you on purpose? She lived in town a couple of years. You'd think word would have gotten out that she was Scarborough's niece."

Sawyer shook his head with a long exhale. "If Dora Yanovich didn't catch wind of it, no one knew. So it had to be a secret on purpose... which still doesn't make sense."

"She wasn't just ashamed of her mother, then, but of her entire family."

"Remember when she moved to town, though," Kade put in. "Right on the heels of Cheri going public about Dillon being Harmony's father and how he'd chased her across a dozen states. It wasn't a good time to align with the family. People wouldn't have welcomed her so much. Paul only got through that time because he's the only real estate agent in town and because he shrugged it all off."

Sawyer grimaced. "That man finds a lot of things mildly amusing, like all of Saddle Springs is a drama put on for his personal benefit."

"So we've established Paul's and Dora's characters." Dad cleared his throat. "Moving on. Does any of that give any clues as to what's held Anna back?"

"I can't think of anything." Sawyer slumped in his seat. "I can't help but believe it's all related, but I still can't put my finger on the pieces or click them together."

"Maybe she thinks if we know about her family connections, we will automatically reject her," ventured Mom.

Kade shook his head. "I don't think so. Not after Cheri. If she's seen anyone in this family withhold love from Cheri or Harmony because of their connection to Dillon, it's far more than I've seen."

"Is Paul's wife on drugs?" asked Trevor. "I'm not asking for the sake of gossip. Just trying to figure this out."

"I haven't heard rumors." Dad looked thoughtful. "But then, I try not to wallow in what I hear, either."

"So what do we know?" Kade placed his hands on the table, palms up. "Anna thinks you're hot but won't marry you. In fact, she ran away from you. She's Dillon's cousin. Her mother might be on drugs and took an instant dislike to you, probably premeditated. Anything else?"

It didn't sound like much, but it was more than he'd had this morning. Of course, this morning he'd expected to see her tonight. Had expected to try to sneak a kiss and make another plea to make her a permanent part of his life, even though she'd made it clear she wouldn't change her mind.

What had really happened the other day? She'd acted so strangely in the barn office, and then he'd blown everything with his ultimatum.

Stupid Sawyer.

"Let's take it to the Lord." And Dad launched directly into a heartfelt prayer.

If only Sawyer could become a man like his father.

CHAPTER 23

Olive hadn't pushed for information all through dinner. Not that Anna had forgotten why her mentor had come, but where should she even start? Finally, Olive curled up at one end of the sofa with a cup of tea, and the room lay silent.

Anna clenched her own cup. "It's a long story."

Her friend took a sip. "We have time."

"My mom... she's always been a mess. Her mother wasn't any better. Men on a revolving door. The inability to keep a decent job. Lots of drinking. Lots of drugs." She took a deep breath. "Lots of debt."

Olive nodded. "Those are hard patterns to break."

There it was. Patterns. Hard, but maybe not impossible? Please, God. "I got in trouble a lot. Ran away. Quit school."

"It must have been difficult."

"It was. Mostly, I've tried to forget. And I tried to stay away from my mother. She saw me as a chance to make money to support her habits. I'm thankful she didn't manage to sell me. Seriously, an overheard conversation was why I ran the first time."

"Oh, no."

"I didn't see her for a few years. Then she found me and came around. She was sorry and all that. She was trying to change her life. I bought into it. Overjoyed to start fresh." Anna's tears dribbled faster until they became a stream. Oh, how naive she'd been. How desperately she'd wanted to believe her mom.

"How long did it last?"

"Not long. I was a cocktail waitress downtown, earning enough steady income for the first time in my life that I qualified for credit cards. I was elated. I know that's dumb. Even then I knew it wasn't free money, that I'd have to pay it back, but it felt like free money, you know? I stupidly shared my excitement with my mother as I applied for one, then another, then a third. I figured if they'd keep offering them to me, I'd keep taking them."

Olive winced.

Yeah, Anna should have winced, too, but she hadn't. Not at the time. "Only the cards never came. After a couple of weeks, my mom wafted back out of my life. That didn't really surprise me, but I didn't think anything of it other than a slight sense of disappointment. It wasn't until the bills began arriving that I realized what had happened."

"She'd intercepted the cards."

"Yes. And I was suddenly fifty grand in debt."

Olive's eyes widened. "How many did you order?"

"I was so naive." Anna buried her face in her hands.

"Some companies counted the cards as stolen and didn't hold me responsible, but others did. My wages were garnisheed. Then I lost my job because my boss didn't want such a loser around. My debt was piling up, and I had no way to pay it."

"Oh, honey."

"My uncle — my mother's brother-in-law — offered to help me find a job in Saddle Springs, so I moved there. Right then his family was undergoing a scandal of its own, and I didn't want anyone to know I was related to them. I wanted to shuck anything to do with my relatives. Uncle Paul agreed to keep the secret. He's an odd sort of man. I think he agreed because he's amused by knowing things other people don't."

"That sounds strange."

"Strange is a polite word for him. He's... well, he stays just on the correct side of the law in his real estate business, but he's willing to dip a little in the shady side if he thinks he can get away with it."

"What happened then?"

"Well, this was three years ago. I was breaking under the weight of the payments to the credit card companies. I couldn't find my mother. Honestly, I wasn't sure I wanted to. What kind of parent does this to her kid?" She rubbed her belly. *Sorry, little one.*

Olive took another sip of tea. "Is that why you've been so determined to give your baby up for adoption?"

Anna blinked back tears, though it was likely a lost cause. "That's a big part of it." She hesitated. Should she finish with the story or take this opportunity to clarify the

Bible's stance on parental sin? "Also, I took *The Merchant of Venice* in junior English class."

The older woman's eyebrows drew together in surprise. "Didn't we all? But I'm not sure what that has to do with anything."

"There's that bit in Act Three where Jessica says, 'So the sins of my mother should be visited upon me.' Launcelot answers, 'Truly then I fear you are damned both by father and mother. Well, you are gone both ways.'"

Olive's mouth opened, but Anna rushed on. "I searched for the reference a few weeks ago to see if anyone had countered Jessica's claim, and you know what I found instead?"

"Tell me."

"Shakespeare didn't make that up. It's in the Bible, too. Several places."

"Honey, did you read the context? Did you study the concept further?"

Anna thought back to the desperation of that November night. Her thoughts had spiraled with her discovery, and she'd become more determined than ever not to embroil either Sawyer or their child in the family curse.

Olive's voice softened. "Did you pray about it? Ask God to show you what it meant?"

"No." Anna was ashamed to admit it, but tonight she wasn't holding anything back. "I thought it was clear."

"Then let me share with you. First, yes, there are scriptures that refer to a generational curse. In Exodus, God presents Himself to Moses in this way. Let me look it up."

Olive tapped her phone several times. "Here we go, in chapter 34. 'The Lord, the Lord, the compassionate and gracious God, slow to anger, abounding in love and faithfulness, maintaining love to thousands, and forgiving wickedness, rebellion and sin. Yet he does not leave the guilty unpunished; he punishes the children and their children for the sin of the parents to the third and fourth generation.' Is that what you read?"

"Similar, but I don't think it was that one. But how does that add up? He says He forgives, but in the next breath He talks about punishing children for something their parents did."

"He's talking about natural consequences. You know how Adam and Eve sinned back in the beginning? Even though it wasn't our fault, we still suffer the repercussions of that. And, yes, the culture of sin is definitely passed on. Kids definitely suffer from their parents' choices, whether it's an absentee father, a parent with addictions, or other patterns."

"Yeah. For sure." Just look at her mother.

"But God makes it clear in Ezekiel 18, where He says, 'What do you people mean by quoting this proverb about the land of Israel: *The parents eat sour grapes, and the children's teeth are set on edge*? As surely as I live, declares the Sovereign Lord, you will no longer quote this proverb in Israel. For everyone belongs to me, the parent as well as the child — both alike belong to me. The one who sins is the one who will die.'"

"But we've all sinned, so we all deserve to die. That's in the Bible, too."

"It is." Olive nodded. "But each person makes a decision what to do with that information on their own. You won't be judged on your mother's choices. Only on your own."

Any hope bubbling up was firmly squashed. "But I've made terrible decisions."

"And you've asked God to forgive you. He has, and He will continue to. Here..." Olive poked at her app again. "Romans 8 starts off, 'There is now no condemnation for those who are in Christ Jesus, because through Christ Jesus the law of the Spirit who gives life has set you free from the law of sin and death.'"

Set free. Why hadn't Anna seen that before? What had she thought Jesus had done for her that night in September when she'd prayed for salvation? She'd gotten caught up in fixing just this one thing... and then that one... before she was good enough for God. "Jesus died for my sins. To forgive me and give me eternal life." She put the pieces together as she spoke. "I think... my habits were so ingrained I added salvation on top of trying to figure things out on my own." How lame was that?

"It's a common thought process, honestly."

Olive was nice enough not to shove in Anna's face that if she'd hung around a bit longer, learned more of the scripture before hightailing it to confront Sawyer and becoming trapped in his ultimatum, she would have learned these things. But, no. She'd hared off, certain she knew the answers.

"Here, listen to this. It's the Apostle Paul speaking to the Galatian church. They were guilty of adding their own works on top of God's grace as though it made any difference. Paul called them foolish and asked who had bewitched them! 'Before your very eyes Jesus Christ was clearly portrayed as crucified. I would like to learn just one thing from you: Did you receive the Spirit by works of the law, or by believing what you heard? Are you so foolish? After beginning by means of the Spirit, are you now trying to finish by means of the flesh?'"

The words were so blunt she could take offense... if the hope didn't shine through them.

"Galatians is a short book, only six chapters, but it's packed with goodness. Chapter 5 starts out like this: 'It is for freedom that Christ has set us free. Stand firm, then, and do not let yourselves be burdened again by a yoke of slavery.'"

Stand firm? Stay free? That all sounded like heaven. Literally and figuratively. Why hadn't she seen it before? In typical Anna fashion, she'd seen a problem and tried to fix it herself. No one had ever stood up for her before. Had ever come alongside and given her a helping hand because they loved her and wanted only her best, no strings attached.

Jesus had done that for her on the deepest of levels, in the core of her being. And she'd, what, thumbed her nose at Him and said, *thanks, I'll take it from here*?

Sawyer. He'd done it for her, too. Not as perfectly or deeply as Jesus, but he loved her. Wanted her. Wanted a family with her, while her guilt had run so deep that she couldn't let down her guard and allow him in.

Her phone dinged with an incoming text. She braced

herself and glanced over. Yes, it was Sawyer. On the lock screen, all she could see was *Anna, we need to talk.*

Fear flared, as familiar as her own breath.

"What's up?" asked Olive quietly.

"I don't know what to say to him."

"There's no need to do anything in haste, honey. May I share some more scripture first? And I think it would be very beneficial if we spent some time in prayer before you contact him."

"He's been so patient with me." Anna's voice broke. "I don't know how much more he'll put up with. How long he'll wait."

"God's got it. He really does."

The phone chimed again. *I met your mother.*

Panic clawed at Anna's throat, and her vision swam. "It's too late," she whispered. "He knows everything."

Sawyer was only human. More patient than many, but even he had his limits. She envisioned his piercing dark eyes gazing into her dark soul and turning away from her. Why did it matter, when she'd been rejecting him all along?

And yet, somehow, it did.

God, why? How do I get out of this mess?

CHAPTER 24

She hadn't replied.

All that night, Sawyer had tossed and turned and prayed. All the next day, he'd prayed and worked. Then another night of intermittent sleep.

Where was God? Why had the sole word he'd sensed been *wait*? He hated waiting. Only remembering that his own impatient ways had not worked kept him in check. Kept him praying as he stood by.

Now he drove the tractor so the bale fork stabbed deep into a round bale. He tilted the bale up a little then drove out to the feeding station. With the hay poised above the feeder, he cut the twines holding it together, then lowered the bale.

Cattle shoved at each other for access to the stanchions, the boss cows winning out. But there'd be enough for everyone once Sawyer had completed the chore and filled all the feeders.

He kept an eye on their general health as he worked. Calving would start in a few weeks, so many of the cows had rounded bellies. But that only made him think of Anna, and the cycle of his thoughts rotated once again.

Wait. Trust.

Lord, I trust. There's nothing else I can do.

His conscience jabbed him along with the bale fork poking into the next bale. Now trusting was a last resort? Something to do when Sawyer had come to the end of his own plans?

I'm sorry. You are God. I'm not. I can't see the big picture, but You can. He remembered the view out the plane window as they flew over the mountains. Routes that had been discovered by the early explorers through many months — sometimes years — of trial and error and hardship and backtracking could have been mapped out in mere minutes from the sky. From a loftier perspective, everything became so very clear. So obvious.

Ah, right. That was even in the Bible. Isaiah 55, wasn't it? *"For my thoughts are not your thoughts, neither are your ways my ways,"* declares the Lord. *"As the heavens are higher than the earth, so are my ways higher than your ways and my thoughts than your thoughts."*

Wasn't that the chapter that went on to say something about God's Word not returning to Him empty? Everything had a purpose. The people of Israel and Judah had been in a rough spot in Isaiah's time as the Assyrian army advanced toward them. Far more had been at stake than Sawyer's current problems with a woman who refused him at every turn. He faced no international consequences.

That didn't diminish his problems, just put them into perspective. With a lighter heart, he hauled as much hay as the cows needed before parking the tractor.

Max, the hired hand, looked up from tinkering with one of the heated automatic waterers. "Thanks for filling in, boss."

"No problem." Sawyer poked his chin toward the valve assembly. "Getting it figured out?"

"Yeah, just needed a new gasket. I'll have it back together pretty quick now."

"Thanks. I guess it's easy when you know how."

Max flashed a grin. "That's the way of most things in life."

"True enough." Sawyer punched the guy's shoulder and headed toward the house.

Christmas Eve. He'd never been away from Eaglecrest at Christmas, no matter how busy or independent he'd gotten. Some days just demanded family. And, now, while his parents and brothers would be around him, he'd be missing the person most important to him. Anna.

He should drive to Bozeman. He could be there before it was too late to knock on Anna's door. He could spend Christmas Eve with her. If she let him.

Wait.

Sawyer didn't want to be patient, but being in a hurry had done him no good. *You've got it, God. I'm waiting.*

He was done fighting it. She'd have to be in touch sooner or later.

Or maybe not.

He'd have to live with that, too, if that's what

happened. Over and over and over again, he'd put Anna and their baby in God's hands.

He rounded the corner of the barn and glanced to the front of the garage where Anna's car had often been parked for the past couple of months. It wasn't there, of course, but the space was plowed. Kade had come early this morning to push last night's snowfall out of the way. The highways department's plow had arrived much later and didn't clean up the yard anyway.

In the distance, he heard a vehicle churning up the long drive. Anna? His heart skipped a beat. No, it was likely his sister-in-law. Cheri's car sounded a lot like Anna's. Still, he paused outside with his gloved hand on the doorknob, just to make sure. Call him an eternal optimist.

Still, his eyes must be deceiving him, because Cheri's car was gray, not white. Anna. She was here.

Sawyer needed to breathe. Needed to do more than stare as she parked her car in front of the door to the garage apartment.

What did it mean? His heart knew what he wanted it to mean, for sure, but was that reality?

God? Please, please help me not to bungle this. Please.

He pulled his hand from the doorknob and came down the steps to the yard as she exited the vehicle. She gathered her hair in one hand and smoothed it over her shoulder as her eyes found his across the top of the car. Locked on.

Sawyer stopped a few feet away, barely daring to breathe. "Anna?"

"Hi." She offered a quick smile then bit her lip. "I've

got some things to say to you. Did I catch you at a bad time?"

He looked down at his chore clothes. Tufts of hay clung to his parka, and smears of dirt — or worse — had permeated his jeans. No doubt he also smelled a treat.

"Go ahead and have a shower. Come find me when you're done." She looked down. "Unless... unless you've changed your mind about me."

Hope bubbled up and over. Sawyer took a few steps closer as he pulled off his gloves. With one finger he lifted her chin until her hazel eyes, full of tears, looked into his. "I'll never change my mind about you."

"You haven't heard me out yet."

He caressed her cheek. "I don't need to. You know what I realized a couple of days ago?"

Anna shook her head slightly.

"I've never told you something very important. I guess in my pride, I thought you knew. But, sweetheart? I love you, Anna Winter. I. Love. You."

Her eyes glistened.

He wanted nothing more than to gather her close and kiss her to demonstrate, but he really did need that shower. He kissed his finger and pressed it to her lips. "Give me fifteen minutes, and I'll be back. You'll wait?"

Anna nodded, and he tore himself away.

After gathering his parents to pray and having the quickest shower of his life, Sawyer strode back across the yard. Dusk had fallen, but the lights of the little Christmas tree shone through the upper window, welcoming him.

He kicked off his boots at the bottom of the stairs then climbed up to the apartment, where Anna waited on the other side of the little island. He got the message. *Distance. Hands off.* She needed to say her piece, and he'd let her, but it changed nothing.

Anna walked into the living room and perched on the edge of one of the chairs. "How was Texas?"

Seriously? "Okay. Hard." He didn't want to think about Ace. He wanted to think about his future with Anna.

"You mentioned once about Ace's girlfriend..."

Sawyer's brow furrowed. Why was she going there right now? "She got what she wanted. Ace's money. Everything he had." The cowboy hadn't had a legal will. That was something Sawyer needed to consider doing, actually.

"I'm sorry."

"Me, too, especially since it left his mom with nothing." He watched Anna as she twisted the hem of her long-sleeved T-shirt. He'd bought her that one two months ago, but it was the first time he'd seen it on her. The baby took up more room beneath it than a week ago. "Anna? Why are we talking about Vanessa?"

She sucked in a big breath, glanced at him, then away. "Because I'm guilty, too."

Surely, he hadn't heard her whispered words correctly. "Guilty? Of what?"

"I was in a desperate place in June. I was under crushing debt because of my mom... but why isn't important. I used you, Sawyer. I *wanted* to become pregnant. I wanted to have a rich guy who could bail me out of my financial problems and make it so I could cut ties with my mother forever. Be free of her and live a life of ease."

Sawyer opened his mouth. Closed it again. Tried to make sense of what she was saying.

"I was no better than Vanessa. When I knew I was pregnant, I went back to Bozeman. I was going to find you at the right time and... oh, Sawyer, this is so hard."

"Keep talking." Had he managed to keep his voice steady? Because his equilibrium was shot. The rug pulled from beneath his feet. He'd thought he'd chosen her, that the attraction had been mutual. Not that he'd been a target.

"But then, in September, I heard about Jesus. Even before that, I knew what I'd done was wrong. Not just the, the sex, but the manipulation. I couldn't go through with it. All I could think of was to give the baby away so I'd be — I don't know, absolved."

A vice clamped around Sawyer's head. Another around his heart.

"The Sawyer I knew in June... I thought he'd be fine with it. It never occurred to me that you'd have a different opinion. That you'd want me and the baby in your life."

"You guessed wrong." He stared hard at her. "I'd *never* have been okay with signing away my child."

Anna's hands twisted in her lap. "I'm sorry, Sawyer. For everything. I know you can't forgive me, but I couldn't keep the truth from you any longer. I'll pack up and leave at first light. I-I'll keep the baby. You can see it sometimes. We'll work out the details." Her lips quivered, and he could see trickles of moisture on her cheeks.

He surged to his feet and paced toward the window,

staring out past the tree at the parking area lit by a few yard lights. What was he supposed to do with all this? He'd said that whatever she told him changed nothing. He'd told her he loved her. Did he? Really? How big was love supposed to be?

His shirt sleeve caught on the little star he'd painted as a child. *Wise men still seek Him.* He looked at the porcelain rocking horse, at the angel bringing messages of peace and good will to a troubled world, at the little cowboy faces laughing from the horseshoe frames.

Christmas was a time to celebrate God's love to the human race. What Anna had done was bad. Sure, it was. But compared to the many ways humans had thumbed their noses at God? Not so terrible.

He turned to look at her, but she was focused on her baby bump, her hair curtaining her face.

Sawyer squatted in front of her and gathered her cold fingers in his. "Anna? Tell me the rest. Why did you leave the other day? Was it because I threatened to raise the baby myself? What happened since?"

"You told your brother you couldn't forgive Vanessa for what she did to Ace." Her voice broke. "In that moment, I knew there was no hope for us. I knew I couldn't hold my secret forever. I knew you'd hate me when you found out, and I couldn't bear it."

So much depended on saying the right thing, right now. "Sweetheart, I am not perfect. I'm pretty sure that's not a surprise to you."

Her mouth pursed, but she didn't look up.

"I've always suffered from an extravagantly sized ego. I spent years humoring myself and living for myself. God has been working on me about that. School of hard knocks." He rubbed his thumbs over her hands as he shot up a quick prayer for guidance. "God has forgiven me for all the running, all the selfishness, all the ego. Everything. How can I not forgive you?"

Anna peered at him through teardrop-laden lashes.

"Sweetheart. I've been falling in love with you ever since June, but especially since our snow day at Kade and Cheri's. I love you. I can't see that changing."

Sawyer rocked back on his heels and pulled them both to standing. He looked down into Anna's hazel eyes, their hands entwined, their baby pressed between them.

Anna searched his face.

He waited, forcing himself to take even breaths, forcing himself to be as patient as she needed.

"Sawyer? I'm a mess. I have so much to learn."

"We're all in that boat."

"My mom..."

He quirked a grin. "I've met her, remember? We'll stand together. We'll figure things out."

"Do you really love me?"

"Anna. Sweetheart. I love you more than life." He pressed a kiss to her forehead.

"I love you, too." She looked up at him.

Sawyer slid his arms around her, one hand sliding up to tangle in her hair as he kissed her. This. This was like coming home.

Oomph. Something jabbed his gut, and he pulled back

with a laugh. "Baby's got something to say about all this." He shifted his hands to caress Anna's belly.

Her hands covered his. "This baby would like a mommy and a daddy who love her and teach her to follow Jesus."

"That can be arranged." Sawyer reached to kiss Anna. "But you meant *him*."

CHAPTER 25

Christmas morning. Anna stretched languidly in the king-size bed in the garage apartment then curved her hands around her belly. "Good morning, baby," she whispered. "Your daddy thinks you're a boy. I hope he won't be too disappointed when he finds out otherwise." Not that she knew for sure. It was just a niggling thought that wouldn't go away.

The baby moved, pressing an appendage to her bladder.

So much for waking up slowly and savoring the memory of Christmas Eve with Sawyer. They'd curled up on the sofa in front of the Charlie Brown tree with hot chocolate and popcorn and talked until the wee hours before he'd headed back across the yard.

He loved her. Forgave her. Promised to pay off her mother's debt.

She loved him.

The thoughts circled round and round as she prepared

for a day with his family. Sawyer's brothers' trucks pulled into the yard then Kade's kids spilled out. From the window, Anna watched Sawyer exit the house, toss a squealing Jericho into a snowbank, squat in front of Harmony for a quick hug, and tickle little Donovan. Then he talked to his brothers and their wives for a moment before continuing to the garage.

This man. This family. How could they be hers? She didn't deserve — no. No more of that thinking. Everyone messed up. No one deserved good things, but God gave gifts anyway.

She tugged her boots onto her feet and reached for her jacket as Sawyer opened the door.

"Merry Christmas, sweetheart." Oh, how his eyes caressed her. Warmed her to the core. He helped settle her jacket across her shoulders then his hands went around her belly. His chin settled on her shoulder, his cheek against hers. "Merry Christmas, son of mine."

Anna chuckled. "You might be in for a big surprise." Seeing him with his niece made her think he'd be completely happy with a daughter.

"Might be." He laughed. "Come on. Ruthie has break-fast ready, and then there are gifts all around."

"But I didn't bring anything."

"Anna. You being here is the greatest gift I could ever want."

"Your family—"

"For them, too. Well, maybe not Donovan. He doesn't much care, at least at the moment."

They walked over to the house, hand in hand, and Sawyer held the door for her.

"Miss Anna!" Harmony flung her arms around Anna's middle and squeezed. "The baby kicked my face!" She giggled.

"Must be a boy," Sawyer deadpanned.

Everyone laughed. Denae stepped closer and gave her a hug. "Welcome back, Anna."

"Thanks. Good to see you." But her gaze went to Cheri beyond. Sawyer had told her his family knew everything, but things had been a bit rocky with Cheri all fall.

But Cheri leaned in for a hug. "Merry Christmas, Anna. Forgive me?"

"Forgive *you*? But it's me who—"

"It's me who judged you for being with Dillon without ever asking why on a deeper level. It's me who assumed I knew what was best for your baby."

Anna hugged Cheri back. "You are *so* forgiven. You did it out of love for Sawyer. Maybe even for me."

"Yes. But it was wrong of me."

"It's done. Gone. Okay? I... I want to be friends."

"Thanks." Cheri gave her a little smile. "I'd really like that, too."

Then Sawyer's parents edged Cheri aside and welcomed Anna home.

Home. She liked the sound of that. She liked the sound of this family as they laughed around the breakfast table. As Ruthie served up Eggs Benedict and a fruit salad. As carols played quietly through the sound system. As Jericho and Harmony begged to open presents.

Sitting by the fireplace after breakfast, Russ read the Christmas story from the Gospel of Luke and prayed for the family, each by name. He prayed for her, Anna, thanking God for her.

Yes. Home.

The children tore into their gifts, shrieking with glee at more toy horses, at books, at a new toboggan. And then the adults exchanged small gifts, thoughtfully chosen.

Cheri gave her a white noise system that played lullabies at the flip of a switch. "You'll be thankful. Trust me."

Anna believed her.

Denae's gift was a set of romance novels she'd edited. "One of my favorite authors. I hope you enjoy them."

She would. But she hadn't brought gifts. She'd denied that she'd be at Eaglecrest for Christmas until the very last minute.

Russ began to gather the torn paper and feed it into the fire, a bit at a time.

Sawyer dropped to one knee in front of her chair, brandishing a small jeweler's box. "Sweetheart." His deep dark eyes were not so mysterious right now. They shone with love and hope. "Anna, my love, will you marry me?"

She'd all but proposed to him herself last night. They'd talked of their future as a family together until well past midnight. Still, the official question rocked her world. Anna cradled his dear face between her palms. "Oh, Sawyer, you know I will. I love you." Her gaze dropped to the glistening diamond. "But where did you get that ring?" Because the jewelry store in Saddle Springs certainly had not been open overnight.

He grinned a little bashfully. "I bought it in Amarillo. I thought... I'm not sure what I thought. Maybe that I could bribe you into saying yes with this ring? I was full of stupidity. Full of ego. But I bought it, anyway."

"It's perfect." He wouldn't be the man she loved if he didn't have that measure of overconfidence.

Sawyer slipped the ring on her finger to the sound of clapping, hollered congratulations, and wolf whistles from his brothers. He drew her to her feet, and there, in front of his family, kissed her soundly.

"Oh!" She pulled back. "I do have a gift for you. A gift for everyone, really. Give me a minute?"

"Want me to come with you?"

Anna shook her head. "I'll be back before you know it."

SAWYER FELT like he was holding his breath the whole time Anna was gone, but it couldn't have been more than five minutes. Not even enough time for the children's new horses to be properly introduced to the original herd.

Anna came in, shielding whatever she carried behind her, even going so far as to circle through the kitchen and breakfast room rather than coming directly into the great room. She stood beside the fireplace with her hands behind her back. Her gaze took in each person in the room then latched onto his.

This was more than a bag of candy canes for the kids to share. But what?

Slowly she drew a sheaf of papers out. "Two months

ago I came here, asking Sawyer to sign papers to give our baby up for adoption. I truly thought this would be the best solution for everyone. That he'd be okay with it."

He swallowed hard.

"I was wrong. I wasn't counting on Jesus working in his life. Or mine. I wasn't counting on falling in love with either him or our baby. But... I did. My gift to you, Sawyer, is to ask you to burn these papers. They no longer represent me or my wishes. Jesus changed me. *You* changed me."

Sawyer nearly stumbled as he crossed the room to where she stood. He took the papers from her and, one at a time, crumpled each sheet and tossed it in the flames. He sat on the hearth and watched until every scrap had been burned to ashes.

I Heard the Bells on Christmas Day streamed quietly from the speakers, mingling with the crackling fire. Otherwise, the great room was hushed. Even the kids had stopped playing to watch the drama unfold.

"Anna?" His mom's voice was quiet. "May we pray God's blessings on this child?"

Sawyer looked up to see his beloved nod. He rose and stood behind her, arms encircling her, hands covering hers as they cradled the baby. His family gathered around, each touching her belly, as first Mom, then Dad, then his sisters-in-law and then his brothers prayed for this new life, for this new family.

They were all quiet as they drifted apart. Denae and Cheri headed into the kitchen, and his parents went the other direction. Kade and Trevor settled onto the floor beside the kids' toy ranch.

But Sawyer couldn't bear to release Anna and let the moment go. He never wanted to let go of her again. "Sweetheart?" he whispered against her neck.

"Hmm?" She twisted slightly to look at him, tears shining in her hazel eyes.

"When can I marry you? Please don't say after the baby."

She turned the rest of the way in his arms. "The sooner, the better."

Sawyer liked the sound of that. "Church wedding? Or maybe right here at Eaglecrest."

"Here sounds lovely. Something small. I want to get to know your church and your pastor and everyone, but..."

"New Year's Eve?" He held his breath.

"That soon?" A smile spread on her face. "I could live with that."

"I'll ask Pastor Roland if he'll do the honors." He rubbed his hands on her back. "Do you want to invite your mom? Or the Scarboroughs?"

Anna's brows drew together. "Are you sure? I don't know if I want to, but maybe I shouldn't make a snap decision."

"We can pray about it for a few days."

"Yes. That's a good idea." Her face brightened. "Oh! I need to phone my friend Olive. I want her here if at all possible."

"I'd love to meet her. Thank her."

Sawyer's parents crossed the great room.

"Mom? Dad?" He towed Anna toward them.

"Yes?" Mom looked between them.

"If I can get Pastor Roland, may we have the wedding here on New Year's Eve? I know that's only a week away..."

"A bit less than." Dad laughed.

Mom clasped her hands together. "A party? I love a good party, and this is the best reason I can think of. Count me in. We can probably fit forty or fifty people. Is that enough? I mean, our family alone is—"

Sawyer laughed. "Just hold half a dozen spots for my friends and Anna's. I want Adam here if he can make it. But let me call the pastor first." He glanced at his watch. "Is it rude to interrupt a pastor's Christmas morning?"

"I'm sure Pastor Roland would love to hear from you." Dad grinned. "You two planning to live in the garage apartment for a while at least?"

Sawyer hadn't gotten that far in his thinking yet. He looked at Anna with eyebrows raised. "Sound good?"

"Better than good."

He dropped a kiss to her waiting lips then excused himself to make a phone call.

And maybe pinch himself that this was real. Twenty-four hours ago, all had seemed lost, but God had been at work orchestrating grace.

Grace. There was a good name for a baby girl. Nah. They were having a boy. He was sure of it.

ACKNOWLEDGMENTS

If you've read previous stories of mine, you'll know that cowboy romance is a minor variation on my usual themes of farm-and-garden such as in my flagship Farm Fresh Romance series. The Montana Ranches overlap slightly with both the Garden Grown Romances (part of the multi-author Arcadia Valley Romance series) where Cheri (Mackenzie) Delgado played a small role, and with the Urban Farm Fresh Romance series, where Denae Archibald appears as a friend to Sadie Guthrie in *Raindrops on Radishes*.

Thanks to Elizabeth Maddrey for being Chief Prodder and First Reader as well as a terrific author whose stories I enjoy reading!

I also appreciate my beta readers: Amy, Paula, Karen, and Gretchen. Thanks for loving this new direction, encouraging me, and catching my errors... although I'm sure I managed to leave a few in, even after my fabulous editor, Nicole, had her input. Thanks for sticking with me through all these years and stories, Nicole.

I'm also grateful for the Christian Indie Authors Facebook group and my sister bloggers at Inspy Romance. These folks make a difference in my life every single day. I'm thrilled to walk beside them as we tell stories for Jesus!

Thank you to my Facebook friends, followers, street team, and reader group members for prayers, encouragement, and great fellowship. If you'd like to join other readers who love my stories, please find us at Valerie Comer: Readers Group.

Thanks to my husband, Jim, whose love for me never fails and who encourages me in every endeavor. Thanks to my kids, their spouses, and my wonderful grandgirls for cheering me on. To them, having an author for a mom/grandma is "normal." Imagine that!

All my love and gratitude goes to Jesus, the One who is my vision, the High King of Heaven, the lord of my heart. Thank you. A thousand times, thank you.

Marry Me for Real, Cowboy

CAVANAGH COWBOYS ROMANCE - 1

VALERIE COMER

GreenWords Media

Adam Cavanagh strode across the parking lot, his thoughts clicking right along with his boots on the slick pavement. Was he honestly slinking home like a whipped pup? He'd be right back under his stepfather's grinding thumb once he drove up the ranch road. How could that be an improvement over risking life and limb every time he blasted out of the chute on the back of a bronc?

His decision had been easy ten years ago. Get out. Make it big. Thumb his nose at Declan Cavanagh.

It wasn't so simple now. Not when Declan would throw him into the saddle with a self-satisfied grunt and order him to work like he was a delinquent child. Adam needed Door Number Three. So far, it had failed to materialize.

"Get your hands off me!" a shrill female voice demanded.

Adam tensed, his step faltering. Where was that coming from? He couldn't tell in the darkness.

A low male voice answered. The woman replied more calmly. Firmly.

She must be okay, and it probably wasn't any of his business. Plus, he was starving. Still he hesitated, scanning the parking lot again, but nothing appeared to be happening in any of the pools of light from the street lamps. Nothing besides angling sleet.

Adam shook his head and entered the brightly lit restaurant. He was imagining things. It happened a lot ever since his buddy's nasty accident in the arena with thousands of fans watching.

Please wait to be seated.

The dining room had a few empty tables, and the aroma of fried liver and onion rings wafted his way. His stomach growled. Where was the hostess, anyway?

The door behind him swung open, ushering in the cold November night. Adam glanced over, and his gaze collided with a woman with wild eyes. She wore jeans and a down parka. Cowboy boots on her feet. Good Montana girl. He nodded in approval.

She hesitated, glancing around the restaurant, back through the door closing behind her, then over at Adam.

What was with her? He couldn't help grinning. She was stinkin' cute. If that had been her yelling in the parking lot, he wouldn't mind coming to her rescue one little bit.

She launched at him, and her arms wrapped around his neck. "Pretend you love me. Kiss me."

Who was Adam to argue with an invitation like that? Besides, his arms had already shot around her, mostly to keep his balance from the impact of her slight body.

He kissed her.

She kissed him back. Wow, did she ever.

The door cranked open again. Footsteps. Boots, again. Heavier this time. "Riley! I didn't mean — whoa."

Adam moved his lips over hers for a few seconds longer, but he really needed to see what trouble had arrived on the heels of this thirty-second diversion.

The girl — Riley? — opened her eyes slowly and smiled up at him. "Thanks," she breathed. "You're a lifesaver."

Being her champion sounded good. He pressed his lips to her forehead and looked over her curls to see the guy she'd been escaping from. No way.

"Scotty Erickson?" Adam couldn't keep the disbelief out of his voice. It was probably reasonable to run into people from his past when he was less than an hour from the family ranch, but why did the first guy he saw have to be this dirt-bag? He tightened his arms around Riley. If Scotty wanted a woman who didn't want him back, he'd have to go through Adam to get her.

"You." Scotty all but spat the word. "Let go of my girl. Come on, Riley. Enough stalling. Time to hit the road. It's gonna start snowing soon."

Riley shook her head slightly against Adam's chest.

"Your girl?" Adam managed a sneer in his tone. "Ry, honey, you two-timing me?"

She blinked up at him, her back still to the other guy. "Never."

That sounded promising. "Get lost, Erickson."

Scotty braced his feet.

Adam took a quick scan for a weapon but didn't see

one. The scum wouldn't likely be that stupid. "Hey, did you get a chance to pick up the engagement ring today?" He nuzzled Riley's curls, still eyeing Scotty. "When will they be done resizing it?"

She pulled back.

He got a little distracted by those wide eyes. Oh, and the soft lips. He kissed her again.

"Uh... not yet." She sounded breathless. "Maybe in a few days."

"The sooner the better. I can't wait to make you my own."

Scotty scoffed. "Get in line, Cavanagh."

"We don't want any trouble in here. Do I need to call the police?" A pudgy middle-aged man stood beside the hostess desk, eyebrows raised.

"Not at all. My fiancée and I met here for a peaceful celebratory dinner." Adam jutted his chin toward Scotty. "He was just leaving."

The host hesitated, his gaze ricocheting between them.

Adam turned his back on Scotty and threaded his fingers with Riley's. "If you've got a booth away from the window, that would be perfect. Right, honey?"

"Sure would!" Riley glanced back at Scotty but stayed with Adam as he followed the man to a booth at the other end.

He slid in across from her. Wow, he'd lucked out this evening after all. She was cute as a filly and sassy besides. Too bad kissing was his limit these days.

"Your waiter will be right with you." The man set two

menus at the end of the table. "Can I get you something to drink in the meanwhile?"

Was that a flash of wariness in Riley's eyes?

"Ginger ale and a black coffee, please." Part of that whole new leaf thing. Besides, he needed his wits about him. "How about you, honey?"

"Ice water." She stared at him as though calculating. "With lemon."

The host nodded and stepped away.

Adam flipped open the embossed menu, but the aroma of liver and onions still called his name. None of the other entrees looked more appealing. "What're you having? Order whatever you like."

"Why?" Her elbows plunked on the table. "Why are you buying me dinner and being so nice to me?"

He leaned against the padded seatback. "Why not?"

"I don't even know your name. Or why Scotty seems to know you."

"The name's Adam Cavanagh."

She didn't blink.

Apparently she didn't follow the rodeo circuit. So, she wasn't quite perfect, after all. "My stepdad owns Rockstead Ranch northeast of town. And I may have missed your name, too. Riley...?"

"Riley Dunning." She licked her lips in a nervous gesture. "Born here in Missoula and raised all over the west."

"Riley Cavanagh has a nice ring to it, don't you think?" He might have asked blandly, but his mind was skittering.

Had a third option shown up, after all? There might be more than one way to shake up things at Rockstead.

"You're some kind of crazy."

Adam belted out a laugh. "You're the one who asked a complete stranger to kiss her."

ONE MINUTE RILEY was trying to ditch Scotty's slimy attention and the next she sat across from a hot cowboy in an upscale restaurant with carte blanche to order what she wanted.

She'd see if he meant it. Who knew when she'd eat again?

When the waiter returned, Adam indicated she should order first.

Riley pointed to the menu. "Steak, medium rare, and crab legs. I'll take the baked potato with extra sour cream, and may I have the Caesar salad instead of the house salad?" She looked up at the waiter, avoiding eye contact with Adam.

Here's your chance to back down, buster.

He leaned across the table and tapped the appetizer selections on the facing page. "Sure you don't want a starter to kick off that feast?"

If he was going to be that way about it... Riley met his gaze and locked on. "Go ahead and order for both of us."

Adam nodded and looked at the waiter. "We'll have the nacho platter first, please. I'll take liver and onions for my entree. Mashed potatoes and double up the gravy. The house salad is fine for me."

"Right away, sir." The waiter gathered the menus and bowed away.

The cowboy narrowed his gaze at her for so long Riley squirmed. "You said I could order anything."

"I did. Meant it, too."

Whew. "Then what's the problem?"

Adam reached over the table and caught Riley's hands. "Tell me how you know Scotty." His hands were strong and rough and tanned, with a thin scar running from his wrist to his thumb.

She resisted the urge to trace it. "He seemed to think I owed him something because I hitchhiked a ride from him."

"What's a nice girl like you doing hitchhiking?"

Riley raised her chin. "Who said I was a nice girl?"

A glimmer of humor shone in his eyes. "The other kind would have considered giving Erickson what he wanted."

"He can't keep his hands to himself."

Adam tipped his head back and chuckled.

What was so hilariously funny? She glared at him before becoming aware of his fingers squeezing hers. Oh. She pulled away, and he let her, though he laughed even harder.

He was so exasperating. And, yes, she owed him. Not only for rescuing her, but for an extravagant dinner.

Exasperating, but such a hunk. The bit of unruly hair peeking out seemed as dark as the Stetson hiding it. His face was strong, angular, and his nose a little crooked like he'd broken it once or twice. His lips... well, she shouldn't be looking at those, because he was an amazing kisser. Like that was any test of a decent human being.

He'd rescued her, though. Kissed her like she'd demanded. Held her tight against his broad, firm chest and sent Scotty packing.

Pretended they were engaged.

Riley shivered.

The waiter set their drinks and the nachos between them.

She reached for a chip and dragged it through the spicy cheese. It tasted even better than it smelled, and that had been amazing.

"Have you eaten today?"

Riley's gaze shot back to Adam's. "Um... not much."

"How come?" He asked it for all the world like he genuinely wanted to know.

She ate three more chips, but his gaze didn't waver. "It's a long story," she said at last. "I doubt you want to hear the details."

Adam's gaze only intensified. "Try me."

"I'm... let's just say I'm between situations and leave it at that." She eyed him. "Besides, I don't know anything about you."

He shrugged. "Already told you where I live. My stepdad operates two of the biggest ranches in the region. My brothers and I will be running one of them when the time is right." He studied her for a long moment.

"What, do I have salsa on my chin?" Riley dabbed with her napkin.

"Not at all. Just thinking... maybe the time is right."

Now he was getting weird. "Pardon me?"

"I've been away a long time. My stepdad and I don't see eye-to-eye on a lot of things, and he hasn't been willing to let me prove myself. I think he'd take me more seriously if I were engaged."

Riley stared at him. "Come again?"

"People break engagements all the time. It doesn't mean a life sentence."

"Wait a minute. You're asking me—"

His phone rang, and he held up one finger to silence her.

It annoyed her like crazy that it worked.

"Yo, Nathaniel. What's up?" Adam took a sip of his ginger ale then set the glass down with a clunk. The ice cubes rattled as his gaze shot back to Riley's. "Erickson's faster than I gave him credit for."

Uh oh. She should have paid more attention to the fact that Scotty and Adam seemed to know each other.

"Yes, that's what he heard ... I didn't tell anyone about Riley because she's a surprise."

Riley snorted.

Laugh lines crinkled around Adam's eyes as he grinned at her. "We haven't made any firm plans yet ... Definitely, bro. You'll be the first to know ... How're things at home? How's Mom?"

He had a mother? He'd talked about his stepfather as though the man were his only parent.

Jaw tensing, Adam looked down at his free hand lining up the cutlery with the edge of the table. "Sorry to hear that ... Riley and I are waiting to be served, so we'll be a couple of hours at least ... Tell Mom I'll see her in the morning then ... You too, bro. Later."

Riley crossed her arms over her chest. "What's going on?"

"Erickson told his sister who told my brother who told my other brother who was understandably surprised since I didn't have a girlfriend yesterday. At least that he knew of."

"Sorry?"

"Don't be."

The waiter chose that moment to set their entrees in front of them. "Can I get you anything else?"

"I think we're good for now." Adam spread his cloth napkin on his lap.

Riley should do the same. She stared at the heaped platter in front of her. The steak was perfectly crisscrossed, and the crab legs joined the beef in sending up a mouth-watering aroma. If she had to get a to-go container later, that would be okay. It'd give her something for breakfast. Best to start with the crab.

She reached for the cracker tool then became aware Adam was still studying her. "What?"

"What are your plans for the next few weeks?"

"Um..." Her mind scrambled, trying to come up with something that sounded believable or important.

"Christmas with your family?"

Right, the holidays were coming. "I don't think so. My parents are..." *Remember how lying was a bad idea?* "Busy this year."

"How are you with horses?"

Riley blinked. "I've ridden some." Not as much as the rich kids she'd known.

"Come with me. We can always use another hand at the ranch. And I need a fiancée until about the new year. What do you say?"

Her jaw dropped as she stared at him. "What's in it for me? Besides you keep your hands to yourself." She couldn't believe for one minute she was entertaining his ridiculous offer.

Amusement glinted in his eyes. "Wouldn't it look odd if I didn't touch my future wife? Besides, she's pretty demanding about being kissed."

A flush crept up Riley's cheeks.

"There will be honest hard work you'll get paid for. A good reference at the other end." He leaned on the table, wholly focused on her. "And did I mention kissing?"

What a preposterous offer. She really ought to laugh him off.

**Marry Me for Real, Cowboy
Cavanagh Cowboys Romance 1
coming Summer 2020**

ABOUT THE AUTHOR

Valerie Comer lives where food meets faith in her real life, her fiction, and on her blog and website. She and her husband of over 35 years farm, garden, and keep bees on a small farm in Western Canada, where they grow and preserve much of their own food.

Valerie has always been interested in real food from scratch, but her conviction has increased dramatically since God blessed her with four delightful granddaughters. In this world of rampant disease and pollution, she is compelled to do what she can to make these little girls' lives the best she can. She helps supply healthy food — local food, organic food, seasonal food — to grow strong bodies and minds.

Valerie is a *USA Today* bestselling author and a two-time

Word Award winner. She is known for writing engaging characters, strong communities, and deep faith laced with humor into her green clean romances.

To find out more, visit her website www.valeriecomer.com where you can read her blog, and explore her many links. You can also find Valerie blogging with other authors of Christian contemporary romance at Inspy Romance.

Why not join her email list where you will find news, giveaways, deals, book recommendations, and more? Your thank-you gift is *Promise of Peppermint*, the prequel novella to the Urban Farm Fresh Romance series.

http://valeriecomer.com/subscribe

www.ingramcontent.com/pod-product-compliance
Lightning Source LLC
Chambersburg PA
CBHW050720180626
46814CB00002B/529